HIRED GUN

"You know who Clint Adams is?" Leo Dorsett asked.

"Yes," Pullman said.

"He's the Gunsmith—"

"I said I know who he is." Pullman had worked for Dorsett since he first opened The Dream Palace, and he'd done everything he'd been asked—and paid—to do. However, he never failed to irk Dorsett with his apparent inability to call him "Mister" Dorsett. "Is he in town?"

"Yes," Dorsett told him.

"Does it look as if he's going to be a problem?"

"I had a problem last night."

"I heard. Somebody killed one of your girls. You think it was Adams?"

"I don't know who it was, but I want you around in case they try again. I also want you around in case I do have some trouble with Clint Adams."

Pullman thought that over for a few moments. "That would be interesting . . . "

DON'T MISS THESE
ALL-ACTION WESTERN SERIES
FROM THE BERKLEY PUBLISHING GROUP

THE GUNSMITH by J. R. Roberts
Clint Adams was a legend among lawmen, outlaws, and ladies. They called him . . . the Gunsmith.

LONGARM by Tabor Evans
The popular long-running series about U.S. Deputy Marshal Long—his life, his loves, his fight for justice.

McMASTERS by Lee Morgan
The blazing new series from the creators of Longarm. When McMasters shoots he shoots to kill. To his enemies, he is the most dangerous man they have ever known.

SLOCUM by Jake Logan
Today's longest-running action Western. John Slocum rides a deadly trail of hot blood and cold steel.

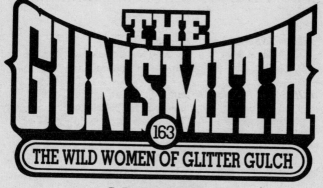

THE GUNSMITH

163

THE WILD WOMEN OF GLITTER GULCH

J. R. ROBERTS

JOVE BOOKS, NEW YORK

THE WILD WOMEN OF GLITTER GULCH

A Jove Book/published by arrangement with
the author

PRINTING HISTORY
Jove edition/July 1995

All rights reserved.
Copyright © 1995 by Robert J. Randisi.
This book may not be reproduced in whole
or in part, by mimeograph or any other means,
without permission. For information address:
The Berkley Publishing Group, 200 Madison Avenue,
New York, New York 10016.

ISBN: 0-515-11656-4

A JOVE BOOK®
Jove Books are published by The Berkley Publishing Group,
200 Madison Avenue, New York, New York 10016.
JOVE and the "J" design are trademarks
belonging to Jove Publications, Inc.

PRINTED IN THE UNITED STATES OF AMERICA

10 9 8 7 6 5 4 3 2 1

ONE

Glitter Gulch was new to Clint Adams.

As he rode down the main street of the town, he was very interested—and amazed—to see how fully it had sprung up where once there was nothing.

This was the usual route Clint took whenever he rode from Texas to California—specifically San Francisco. As far back as earlier in the year this area had been deserted, with no buildings in sight at all. Now, suddenly—or seemingly so—there was Glitter Gulch.

The buildings were all spanking new and clean, and the streets were clear of holes, stones, and the like. There was a bustle of activity—people coming in and out of stores, crossing the street back and forth—and Clint found it equally amazing that there were already so many people living in town.

He rode to the end of the street, where the livery was, and dismounted.

"Howdy," the liveryman said, coming out to meet him. He was young, clean-cut in appearance and dress, and smiling widely. "Welcome to Glitter Gulch."

"Thanks," Clint said.

"My name's Tim," the young man said. "Be stayin' with us long?"

"I'm not sure," Clint said. "To tell you the truth, I didn't know this town was even here. I thought I still had another fifty miles to go to Woodland."

"Ain't no more Woodland. After us you got about a hundred and fifty miles to go to the next town."

"I see."

"We ain't just a stopover the way Woodland was, though. People come here, they generally stay for a while."

"I can understand why they might do that," Clint said. "Glitter Gulch looks like a fast-growing place."

"That it is, mister. Once you see what we have to offer, you won't want to leave for a while."

"Is that so?"

"It sure is."

Clint thought the young man was inordinately proud of his town. Were the other residents the same way? What exactly did Tim mean when he mentioned what the town had to offer?

"That's a great-lookin' horse," Tim said. "Can I take him for ya? I'll take good care of him."

"That's what I'm here for," Clint said, handing

him Duke's reins. Why else would he be here? "Careful with him. He gets ornery sometimes."

"I can handle him. Horses like me."

That was true of most men who worked with horses for a living—not that horses necessarily liked them, but that the men knew how to handle the animals.

"How long do you think you'll be stayin'?" the man asked.

"My intention was to just stay overnight," Clint said, "but maybe I'll add another night, since you're so proud of this town of yours."

"You'll see, mister," Tim said. "You're gonna like it here . . . a lot!"

Clint took his saddlebags and rifle from Duke's back and allowed Tim to lead the big gelding into the livery. Tim told him they'd settle up when he was ready to leave town. That surprised him.

"How many hotels does your town have?"

"Two," Tim said, "but we're building another one. In fact, we're building another whole street at the north end, and that's where the new hotel's gonna be."

"Well, right now I need a hotel that's already standing," Clint said. "Which would you suggest?"

"It don't make no difference," Tim said. "They're both the same."

"I see."

"Just walk back the way you come and you'll see them. They're on different sides of the street, though."

"Okay, thanks."

"And you'll want to make sure you see our

entertainment later tonight."

"The saloons, you mean?"

"Oh, sure, the saloons, but we got theaters, too, with music."

"Is there gambling?"

"There's gambling everywhere," Tim said. "Whatever your pleasure is—faro, roulette, black-jack, poker—you name it."

"Well, that's the kind of entertainment I like," Clint said. "What about women?"

Tim smiled widely and said, "Just you wait!" And that's all he said.

"Well, thanks for your help," Clint said.

"Sure, anytime, and don't worry about your horse. I'll take good care of him."

"I'm sure you will."

Clint tossed his saddlebags over his left shoulder and, carrying his rifle in his left hand, started back the way he had come on Main Street.

TWO

Clint noticed something odd as he walked toward the town's two hotels. He passed people with pleasant expressions on their faces, and people with rather pinched, unhappy looks on their faces. That in itself was not unusual. What *was* unusual was that all of the pleasant looks were on the men and the unhappy looks were on the women.

He stopped at the first hotel he came to and walked into the lobby. He could hear the sound of voices and gaming coming from the hotel saloon as he approached the front desk. There was a doorway with batwing doors which obviously led into the saloon.

"Afternoon, stranger," the desk clerk greeted.

"Good afternoon."

The man was tall and sandy-haired, wearing wire-frame glasses and a dark suit and tie. He was approaching forty, and his hair was beginning to thin in the front. He didn't look concerned, though. In fact, he looked very friendly and happy.

"Just ride in?"

"That's right."

"Well, we appreciate you stopping here for a room. How long do you intend to stay?"

"I haven't decided."

"Well, sign the register and I'll give you a real nice room."

Clint put his saddlebags down on the desk.

"Is a nice room an expensive room?" Clint asked, signing his name.

The man smiled broadly and said, "All the rooms cost the same, friend, but if you want a specific size—"

"No, no," Clint said, pushing the register back across the desk, "a nice one will do."

Clint was amazed at the good humor both the liveryman and the desk clerk were in. In the past he'd noticed that since both types of men usually met people who were on the move, and they were stuck in their jobs—their lives—they were not always pleasant people. In Glitter Gulch, however, this did not seem to be the case.

Clint accepted his key to room twelve and picked his saddlebags up off the desk. As he was turning, he heard men shouting from the saloon.

"Sounds lively," he commented.

"It is," the clerk said.

"Gambling?"

"Oh, yes," the clerk said, "there's gambling in all of the saloons in town."

"How many would that be?"

"Three saloons," the man said, "and then each

of the hotels has its own."

"That's a lot of saloons."

"There are also, uh, other places with gambling in them," the man said, "and fine entertainment. You'll find out about those, if you look hard enough."

"Well, maybe I will," Clint said, "but first I'd like a beer and a bath."

"Would you like me to have someone take your things upstairs so you can have that beer? And I can have a bath drawn for you."

"I'll need a clean shirt—"

"You can give me the shirt and it will be there when you take your bath."

Clint thought a moment. He really did need a beer, and this would keep him from having to make a trip up and down the stairs.

"All right," he said.

He put the saddlebags back on the desk and pulled a clean shirt out of one of them.

"There you go."

"How about the rifle?" the clerk asked.

Clint looked down at the weapon, and then said, "I'll hold on to that."

"Whatever you like, sir. I'll have your saddlebags put in your room and your bath drawn. When it's ready I'll have someone come into the saloon to fetch you."

"Thanks."

"Hot or cold?"

"What?"

"Your bath," the clerk said. "Hot or cold?"

"Oh, hot."

"Very well. Enjoy your beer, sir."

"I will."

Clint walked over to the entrance to the saloon and pushed the batwing doors, wondering if the people he'd find on the other side would be as friendly.

THREE

The room was packed, with people bellied up to the bar and the gaming tables. Clint had seen hotels before with their own saloons, but outside of San Francisco and Denver and places like that he'd never seen a hotel with one this large, and this busy.

The bar was on the left, and it ran the length of the wall. Behind it two bartenders were working hard to keep up with their thirsty customers. Scattered around the room were the gaming tables. Clint couldn't see them very well because of the crowd, but he could hear the sound of a small white ball bouncing around on a turning wheel and then coming to rest on a number. He also heard the sound of dice being rolled.

His entrance had drawn very little attention, and for that he was grateful. He walked to the bar and found a space just wide enough for him to fit into.

"What can I get ya?" the bartender asked. He was a portly man, barely five six, and being behind the bar somehow made him seem smaller.

"A beer."

"Comin' up."

Clint was accidently shoved by the man standing next to him. It was the kind of contact that, in a saloon, very often escalated into a fight, no matter who was at fault. This time, however, it was different.

"Sorry, friend," the man said, "didn't mean to bump into you."

"That's all right," Clint said.

"Can I buy you a drink?"

The bartender came with his beer and Clint said, "I already have one. Thanks for the offer."

The apology made and accepted, the offer made and turned down, the man waved a hand and turned back to his friend.

Clint lifted the beer mug and stepped away from the bar to drink it where there was room. He spotted a woman, a blonde in her thirties with creamy skin and too much makeup, coming toward him.

"You look new," she said, smiling.

"I am."

"Can I show you around?"

"It looks pretty crowded," Clint said. "I just came in for a beer before a bath . . ."

"In the hotel?"

He nodded.

"You can get a much better bath here," she said, sizing him up. "Upstairs."

"I think I'll just finish this beer and take my own bath."

"Well, when you're freshened up, honey, come on back in. My name's Nell."

"Thanks, Nell. I will."

She smiled, then turned and walked away to find a more likely prospect.

There were other women working the floor, but the place was too crowded for him to count how many. He saw a tall, slender, dark-haired woman and a tiny, bouncy redhead. Like most places of its kind, the hotel saloon offered women of all sizes and shapes. A man could very likely find any vice to his liking here. At the moment, though, Clint was not interested in a vice, just a beer and a bath.

"Are you Mr. Adams?"

He turned and saw a hotel bellboy standing behind him. "Bellboy" was a misnomer, though. As was the case with many of them, this "bellboy" was about fifty.

"That's right."

"I'm supposed to tell you that your bath is ready."

"Okay, thanks."

"Want me to show you?"

Clint looked at his beer mug and found that it was still half full.

"I'd like to finish this," Clint said. "Why don't you just tell me where to go when I'm ready?"

"Easy," the man said. "There's a hallway to the left of the desk. You go down there, first door on the right is your bath. Towels and soap are there, also your clean shirt."

Clint took two bits from his pocket and passed it to the man.

"Thanks," he said, and went back into the hotel lobby.

Clint took his time with the beer, which was good and cold. He watched the men at the tables exhibit their joys and their sorrows when the wheel or the dice came to a stop, or when their cards were turned up. He was surprised, however, that there were no voices being raised in anger, as there usually were in places like this.

Glitter Gulch was becoming, more and more, a most unusual town.

He finished the beer and placed the empty mug back on the bar.

"How about that drink now, friend?" It was the man who had bumped into him. Refusing a man's offer to buy you a drink was often regarded as a slight. In this case, however, Clint decided to risk it.

"I just got to town, friend. I wanted one beer, and now I've got a bath waiting. If you don't mind, I'll take you up on that another time."

He hoped he had worded it so that no slight could be taken.

"I know how that feels," the man said. "The offer's always open."

"Thanks."

Clint turned and quit the saloon, stepping back into the lobby. He spotted the hallway the bellboy had told him about and headed for it.

FOUR

Leo Dorsett watched as the woman standing in front of him removed her clothing. She did it slowly, teasingly, until she was naked.

"Stand still," he said.

She did as she was told, but she stood with her hands on her hips, looking at him boldly.

She was blond, her hair long and fine. Her shoulders were wide, which was why she was able to carry her full breasts so proudly. She had a slim waist, good hips, and excellent thighs and calves. She had ugly ankles, though, but no one was going to be looking down there, not with a set of breasts as big and round as hers. Also, her nipples were pink. Dorsett knew that he had customers who liked big blondes with pink nipples.

He turned and looked at the woman sitting next to him.

"What do you think?"

April Donovan looked at him, then back at the naked woman. April had long hair like the woman, but dark rather than blond. She was not built anywhere near as big as the blonde. Her breasts were high and firm, not small by any means, and yet this woman made her feel that way.

"She's a cow," she said.

"I know," Dorsett said.

"The men will love her," April said. "Hire her."

"My sentiments, exactly."

The naked woman had not been able to hear their comments.

"Get dressed, honey," Dorsett told her. "You're hired."

"Oh, thank you, Mr. Dorsett."

She had a high-pitched voice, which was her only drawback.

"What's your name?"

"Gladys."

"Do me a favor when you're on stage, Gladys."

"Of course." She frowned. "What?"

"Don't ever speak."

She continued to frown, then smiled hesitantly, then nodded.

"Go outside and see Maisy," April said. "She'll show you where your room is and tell you when you go on."

"Thanks."

Gladys hastily dressed, her flesh jiggling interestingly as she did so. Dorsett decided that he had better interview her in private in the near future—and make sure she didn't speak.

"Any more today?" he asked.

"She was the last one."

"How many did we see?"

"Thirteen."

"How many did we hire?"

"Three."

"Who?"

"This one—Gladys—a redhead named Alice, and the black girl. Her name was Elsa."

Dorsett remembered Elsa. She was a skinny little thing but she had big, round breasts with dark brown nipples. Yeah, he'd need a private interview with her, too.

"Change Alice's name," he said.

"Okay."

"And Gladys. Call her . . . I don't know. You name her."

"Okay. What about Elsa?"

"No," Dorsett said, recalling the light chocolate color of her skin, "leave her alone. Elsa is just perfect."

"Sure," April said.

She started to get up, but Dorsett grabbed her arm.

"Where are you going?" he asked.

He saw just a hint of fear in April's eyes.

"Aren't we done?"

"We're done with the auditions," he said, "but we're not done."

Dorsett was a big man, six two, built solidly, and very strong. April Donovan knew she'd never escape from his grasp unless he let her go.

"You know how I get at these auditions, April."

"I know, Leo . . ."

Suddenly, he released her wrist. It hurt, but she was determined not to rub it.

"Then do it."

"Leo . . . I don't want to . . . not today. . . . "

"April . . ."

"I have a lot of work to do—"

"Maisy can handle it for a while."

"Leo . . . don't make me . . ."

"I'm not making you, April," Dorsett said, "I'm letting you."

"Leo—"

"Do it!"

His shout cut her off and made her jump. She moved from the chair to her knees in front of him and began to undo his trousers. She slipped off his boots, then he lifted his butt from the chair so she could slide his pants and underwear down. He had bathed recently and his body smelled clean, but that was never a problem with Dorsett. He was clean, attractive, and he had a fine body. His penis, fully erect now, would impress any woman.

April leaned over him, her hair falling on his bare thighs, and slid her tongue over the head of his cock. This could have been pleasurable for her if she were doing it voluntarily, but Dorsett never allowed that. He had sex when he wanted it, on his terms, and he allowed no deviation from that.

She closed one hand around the base of his penis and took him into her mouth.

"Oooh, yes, baby," he said, "wet it, make it wet . . ."

She wet him thoroughly with her saliva and then began to suck, moving her head up and down.

"Yes, oh yes," Dorsett said, taking her head

lightly in his hands, "that's good, that's very good. You're so good, April, why do you make me force you to do this? You know you want to do it, don't you? Don't you?"

"Mmm-hmm," she replied, not releasing him from her mouth. If she could get him to come quickly maybe he'd let her leave, but—

"Slower, damn it!" he said. Suddenly, he slid one hand down to her shoulder and pinched her. It hurt and she couldn't help but wince, but she tried not to let him notice. She slowed down.

"That's it," he said, removing his hand, "slowly, I don't want to rush this . . . ooh, yeah, baby, that's it. . . . You're the best, April, the very best . . ."

She closed her eyes and tried to think of something else, tried to block out his voice, his lies, tried not to think of what was going to happen when he was finished. . . .

Her bruises had barely healed from the last time.

FIVE

After his bath—a long, soothing one—Clint went up to his room to make sure his saddlebags had gotten there. He had remained in the bathtub until the hot water turned tepid. The tips of his fingers were wrinkled, but he felt clean and relaxed.

Satisfied that everything that should be there was there he left the room and went to find something to eat.

He stopped at the desk to ask the man for a likely place.

"The food's good here," the clerk told him.

"Where?"

"Here," the man said, "in town."

"You mean anywhere?"

"That's right, anywhere."

Clint couldn't believe it.

"You mean there are no bad restaurants in town?" he asked.

"None."

"And no bad hotels?"

"None."

"And saloons?"

"All good," the clerk said, "with good gambling, and very good entertainment."

"I've been hearing a lot about this entertainment," Clint said. "What's it all about?"

"You'll see. Why don't you go to one of the saloons—"

"Right now the only entertainment I want is a good steak."

"Go into our dining room, then. You'll find what you want there."

"Thanks."

Clint started away, then turned back.

"Does this town have a sheriff?"

"It sure does," the clerk said, "and a good one."

"Who would expect less?" Clint asked.

"Huh?"

"Never mind. What's the sheriff's name?"

"Osborne," the clerk said, "Sam Osborne."

Clint didn't recognize the name.

"Okay, thanks."

"You know him?"

"No," Clint said, over his shoulder, "I don't know him."

As Clint walked into the dining room the clerk frowned. Maybe, he thought, the sheriff would be interested to know who was in town. He looked across the room at one of the bellboys and waved him over.

* * *

Clint was working on his steak when a man entered the dining room. He stopped just inside the door and looked around. While the saloon had been full, the dining room was empty, except for Clint. There could be no doubt who the man was looking for.

The man walked across the room to Clint's table and then moved aside his vest to reveal the badge he wore pinned to his shirt.

"Mr. Adams?"

"Sheriff Osborne, I presume."

"That's right."

"Why don't you sit down and have some coffee?"

"Thanks."

Osborne sat and Clint looked him over while he poured him a cup of coffee. He was fairly young, maybe thirty, but he had some wear on him. Clint was willing to bet that the man had moved around a bit before he settled here as the law.

"What can I do for you, Sheriff?"

"I'm just making a courtesy call on a stranger in town, Adams."

Clint laughed.

"Do all strangers rate these courtesy calls?"

"No," Osborne said, "just the ones with big reputations."

"That means that you have a speech for me."

"That's right."

Clint sat back in his chair, his steak finished.

"Okay, then, you better give it to me."

The sheriff did, without hesitation.

"This is a nice, quiet town, Adams, but it's much more than that."

"So I've been hearing."

"I've got five deputies to help me keep the peace. They're good men."

"I'm impressed," Clint said, "but why so many?"

"Like I said, this is an unusual town. We have some . . . unusual forms of entertainment."

"So I've been hearing," Clint said, "but no one has been willing to tell me much about it."

Osborne stared at Clint for a moment, sipping his coffee, and then said, "It has to be experienced firsthand . . . to be believed."

Osborne put his cup down and stood up.

"That's it?" Clint asked.

"That's all. You're welcome to stay in town as long as you don't cause any trouble."

"I appreciate that."

"If you cause trouble," the lawman added, "you'll have to deal with me, reputation or not."

Clint eyed the man for a moment, then said, "I kind of figured that."

SIX

Clint took his time over the rest of the coffee. The young sheriff had impressed him. He had walked in, drank coffee with him, stated his case and left. Not once had he fawned over Clint's reputation. He didn't find many lawmen like that anymore.

He finished his coffee, paid his bill, and went outside. The street was busy, and people nodded and said hello to him as they passed. Usually, a stranger in any town was looked at suspiciously. This was quite a change.

The dining room had been empty because he'd eaten between lunch and dinnertime. The saloons, however, seemed to be busy all the time. He could hear the sounds coming from the one across the street, and from one in another hotel when he went past it. From somewhere down the street he could hear music. He decided to go and see what all the fuss was about the entertainment in Glitter Gulch.

Leo Dorsett's saloon was called The Dream Palace. He named it that because it catered to man's every dream. He offered beer, liquor, women for all purposes, and gambling. Dorsett was proud of his saloon and thought it was the finest in town. He certainly had the best women, thanks to April Donovan.

April had started out simply as one of Dorsett's string of women, but he quickly recognized the fact that she was as smart as she was beautiful—if not more so. Rather than treat her like the other girls, or take the chance that someone might hire her away from him, he decided to give her more responsibility—but he also decided to take control of her.

Dorsett was a domineering man, especially with his employees. They were paid well to take his abuse, and if they didn't like it they could go elsewhere.

April Donovan, however, was a different story. He paid her more than the others, but he also exerted more than dominance over her, he exerted control. He used violence, fear, and sex. If you kept a woman frightened, you had a good chance of controlling her. If, however, you also kept her humiliated, then she was completely yours.

As intelligent as April was, this had worked with her. Consequently, she remained with Dorsett as his sometimes lover and manager of the girls. She also helped him hire new girls, as they had done today.

Dorsett did not usually sit in the saloon with the

crowd and watch his girls perform, but tonight the three new girls were going on, and he wanted to watch them work. He'd be able to tell from their first time—hell, the first five minutes—whether they would be able to work for him or not.

Dorsett sat at a table against the right wall that was kept reserved for him. Seated to his right was April Donovan, looking lovely in a low-cut blue gown.

Dorsett was dressed entirely in black, looking like the gambler he had been before he came to Glitter Gulch and opened his business.

That's where Dorsett and April were when Clint Adams entered the saloon.

The name intrigued Clint first. The Dream Palace was not a name that could be overlooked easily. It made certain promises that a man was almost forced to wonder about. He went no further and entered.

Inside it was set up like almost any other saloon. But a long, expensive mahogany bar told him it was not run-of-the-mill, as did the silver and gold trim. Even the girls who were working the floor looked a cut above what he usually saw in a saloon. They were lovely, young—none seemed over thirty— and they were smiling. Not just smiling, but apparently happy. To a one their smiles touched their eyes, a rare occurrence in a saloon girl.

There was a small stage toward the back of the room, and Clint assumed that this was where the entertainment would take place.

There was standing room only, so show time was probably very close. He went to the bar and elbowed himself some room.

"What?" the bartender asked shortly.

"Beer."

The man nodded, and his extra two chins kept nodding long after his head had stopped. He was the fattest man Clint had ever seen, but he moved well and the beer was in front of him before he knew it. Clint paid for the beer, picked it up, and turned to look the room over again.

Against the right wall he noticed a man dressed in black and a beautiful blond woman in blue. The thing he found odd was that although they were sitting together, they were not talking. In fact, the woman seemed to be taking great pains not to look at the man.

While Clint watched, however, the man leaned over and said something to the woman. She listened, nodded, then stood up and walked to the small stage, mounting it.

Was she the entertainment? he wondered. If so, it might be worth staying around a while, especially if she just worked for the man in black, and did not belong to him.

The crowd of men started to make noise, sensing what was coming, but when the woman in blue raised both of her hands, a hush fell over them.

She had them in the palm of her hand.

"I know what all you boys are here to see," she said. She didn't speak any louder than what was probably her normal, conversational tone. She didn't have to. A hush had fallen over the whole room.

"I also know you could have gone to any of a

half a dozen other places tonight. You could have gone to Lou Whilson's Golden Nugget."

"He waters his drinks," someone shouted, and the men laughed.

"Oh, I doubt that," the woman said, but her tone said otherwise. "You also could have gone to Molly Haywood's Gold River."

"Her girls are ugly as sin!" another voice called out.

More laughter.

"Well, that may be," the woman said, "but you won't find that problem here."

"We know, that's why we're here!"

"All right, then," she said, "we'll give you what you came for, and a few new girls to boot. First up is one of your favorites. Here's . . . Lisa!"

Lisa turned out to be a tall, busty brunette who came out wearing a filmy garment—if it could even be called that. The piano player started playing and she started dancing. While she was very pretty and well endowed, she didn't dance particularly well. It took several minutes before Clint discovered just what everyone had come there to see.

The woman on the stage leaned over to speak to some of the men, shaking her breasts teasingly. They jiggled and shook, and then she stood up straight, reached behind her and released her top. It fluttered to the floor and the men went wild. Her breasts were large and firm, and the nipples were as dark as a penny. Clint caught himself staring in disbelief and was even more shocked to find that the woman—Lisa—then proceeded to remove the rest of her clothes.

This was entertainment like he'd never seen.

SEVEN

In rapid succession women of varying sizes and shapes—all of them pleasing—came out onstage, danced and removed their clothes—all of their clothes. Clint had never seen anything like it. He had certainly seen women onstage before, but they were acting, or singing, or dancing. This was the first time he had ever seen a woman actually take her clothes off for an audience.

One of the women was something quite special. Tall, blond, full-bodied, she was a better dancer than the others, moving sinuously back and forth across the stage, removing her clothing slowly, teasingly, until she was gloriously naked. She ended her act by palming both of her breasts, as if she was holding them out to the audience as an offering.

When the show was over the men applauded, whooped, and stamped their feet. The first woman, who had introduced each woman in turn—seven in all—stood up again and the men quieted down.

"That's our entertainment for tonight, gentlemen. From the sound of you, I take it you enjoyed it."

The men reacted again, pounding their feet and shouting.

"Then you'll all be back tomorrow?"

The same method of assent.

"Good. Meanwhile the night is young. Drink, gamble, and the girls will be out shortly to . . . mingle?"

Clint watched the woman walk back to the table and sit with the man.

"Bartender?"

"What'd you think?" the barkeep asked. "First time, huh?"

"How did you know?"

"The look on your face," the fat bartender said. "It's always a giveaway. So? Did you? Like it, I mean?"

"Oh, yes," Clint said. "I've never seen anything like it."

"The girls will be out here pretty soon, if you want to meet any of them."

Actually, Clint would not have minded meeting any of those girls, but the one that was really intriguing him was the woman who had hosted the show.

"Who was the woman who did all the talking?" Clint asked.

"You have a good eye for beauty, sir," the bartender said, "but she's not one of the girls. Do you see the man sitting with her?"

"How could I miss him?"

"He's the boss."

"And she belongs to him?"

The barman nodded.

"Very private stock. Like I said, though, the other girls will be out here real soon."

"What's her name?" Clint asked, still looking at the woman sitting with the boss.

"His name is Leo Dorsett," the man said, "and hers is April Donovan."

"Okay," Clint said, "thanks."

The bartender leaned his elbows on the bar.

"A word of advice?"

"Sure."

"Don't even think about her," he said. "The boss will know, and he ain't a pleasant man."

Clint looked at the bartender and said, "I'll keep that in mind."

Clint turned his back to the bar and looked across the room at the woman. As if to prove the bartender right, the man suddenly turned his head and caught Clint's eye. The two men stared at each other for a few moments, and then the other man said something to the woman, stood up, and started across the room.

EIGHT

"Do you know him?" Dorsett asked April.

April looked across the room at the man Dorsett was talking about. She didn't know him, but she found him interesting-looking. She didn't say that, though. It might have been enough for Dorsett to have the poor man killed.

"Never saw him before."

"He seems interested in you."

"I do attract men, Leo," she said.

"Wait here."

He started to get up.

"What are you going to do?" she asked.

He looked at her and said, "Just wait here."

She started to say something else, but Dorsett turned and walked away, heading toward the bar.

Clint watched as the man approached him. Sensing something, the men to either side of him moved away, which created some elbow room, if he needed it.

Dorsett was in his thirties, a tall, well-built man wearing a black gambler's suit. Clint was sure that there was a gun beneath the jacket. Dorsett was either wearing a shoulder rig, or there was a holster built right into the jacket, like Clint had seen Luke Short wear in the past.

Dorsett walked up to the bar next to Clint and said, "Beer, Jake."

"Sure, Boss."

The bartender caught Clint's eye for just a moment, as if reaffirming his previous warning.

Jake put the beer in front of Dorsett, who picked it up and turned to face Clint.

"You're new in town."

"Brand-new."

"How'd you like the show?"

"I liked it a lot," Clint said. "It was very . . . interesting."

"To say the least."

"How long has this kind of entertainment been going on here?"

"In my place? Or in town?"

"Both."

"Actually, about the same time. The town was built around this kind of entertainment, because you can't get it anywhere else, except maybe in Paris, France."

"Have you ever been to France?"

"No, but I heard tell they have this kind of entertainment. You ever been there?"

"No," Clint said, "but I've been to London."

"London, England?"

"That's right."

"What's that like?"

Clint laughed and said, "Not like this."

The conversation was not going at all the way he thought it would when the man first came over. He expected some kind of challenge, since he'd been caught looking at the man's woman. Instead, the man seemed suddenly interested in him, and in places he'd been. He suddenly saw the man in a different light, and could see where women would find him attractive when he was projecting this side of his personality. He had seen only for a moment in the man's eyes the reason for the bartender's warning.

"I've been to San Francisco, and New York, but I've never been out of the country. Where else have you been?"

Clint told him that he'd also been to South America and to Australia.

"Where's Australia?"

Clint told him. More and more the threatening part of Leo Dorsett faded away, and he was becoming almost boyish in his interest.

"Listen," he said to Clint finally, "my name is Leo Dorsett. I own this place. Why don't you come over to my table and join us? I'd like to buy you a drink and, if you haven't eaten, a meal."

"Well . . ."

"I serve the best steaks in town."

Clint *was* hungry.

"All right," Clint said, "you sold me."

NINE

Clint followed Leo Dorsett to his table, where April Donovan was waiting. From the surprised look on her face Clint knew that she hadn't expected him to be coming back to the table.

"April, I want you to meet . . ." Dorsett turned to him and said, "I haven't even asked you your name."

"Clint Adams."

Dorsett turned away, then turned back quickly.

"Clint Adams?"

"That's right."

"*The* Clint Adams?"

Clint was used to this reaction.

"I'm the only one I know of."

"April," Dorsett said excitedly, "do you know who this is?"

"Clint Adams," she said.

"Not just Clint Adams," Dorsett said, "this is

Clint Adams, the Gunsmith."

"Oh," she said.

Clint didn't think she knew who he was, because her reaction was so understated. Dorsett, on the other hand, seemed even more excited by Clint's presence.

"Mr. Adams, this is April Donovan. I'm sure you noticed that she was our hostess for the show."

"Yes," Clint said, "I noticed."

Up close she was even more beautiful.

"Sit, please," Dorsett said, seating himself across from April. That left Clint to sit between them.

"April, I invited Mr. Adams to eat with us."

"I have to go and check the girls," she said.

Clint saw something pass between the two as Dorsett gave her a hard look.

"Then go and check and then come back," the man said. "And come back soon. I don't want to keep our guest waiting."

She gave Clint a look then stood up and walked away.

"Your wife?" Clint asked.

"No. She works for me."

"Is that all?"

Dorsett looked into Clint's eyes and said, "No."

Clint decided not to push it.

"So what are you doing in Glitter Gulch, Mr. Adams?" Dorsett asked.

"Just passing through."

"On your way to where?"

"California."

"What part?"

Clint shrugged.

"San Francisco, Sacramento. I haven't decided yet."

Dorsett looked across the room and waved someone over. A woman—not one of the entertainers—came walking over.

"Steak, Mr. Adams?"

"Sure."

"Two specials, Holly."

"What about Miss Donovan?" Clint asked.

"Oh, yes," Dorsett said. "Three, Holly."

"Sure, Mr. Dorsett."

"And two beers."

"Yes, sir."

Holly was in her thirties, well built but a few years past her better days. Clint and Dorsett watched her walk away.

"Even your waitresses are pretty."

"I only hire good-looking women, Mr. Adams," Dorsett said. "That's why I run the most popular place in town."

"Other places show the same kind of entertainment?" Clint asked.

"Several others, yes, but not the same caliber as here."

"You're modest."

Dorsett laughed.

"I have nothing to be modest about, Mr.—may I call you Clint?"

"Sure," Clint said, "why not. After all, you are buying."

"Yes, I am," Dorsett said.

Holly returned with two beers.

"Your dinners should be here any minute, Mr. Dorsett."

"Thanks, Holly."

Clint sipped from his fresh beer and wondered what he was doing here. Dorsett was a man of substance in Glitter Gulch, which meant he wielded some power. He was probably not the kind of man to be playing games with.

"You should stay in Glitter Gulch awhile, Clint," Dorsett said. "It's a very interesting place, a fast-growing community."

"I can believe it," Clint said. "It wasn't long ago there was nothing on this spot."

"I know that."

"Who was behind the building of Glitter Gulch?"

"Nobody's really sure of that."

"You?"

"Me? Oh no, not me. I heard about it early, though. This was the first saloon to open in Glitter Gulch. The others all came later."

"And this kind of entertainment? Was that your idea?" Clint asked.

"I'd like to take credit for that, but I can't."

"Whose idea was it then?"

"Ah," Dorsett said, "here's dinner."

Holly returned and placed three plates on the table. The cuts of steak took up most of the room on the plates. The rest was occupied by vegetables.

"I hope Miss Donovan gets back before her dinner gets—"

"Here she is," Dorsett said.

Clint turned and saw April approaching the

table. He stood up as she reached them, then sat again after she did.

"Is everything all right?" Dorsett asked.

"Yes."

"How are the girls?"

"They're getting dressed."

"Eat your dinner, April, before it gets cold."

She hesitated, then picked up her utensils, cut a piece of meat, and put it in her mouth. The whole while she kept her eyes on Dorsett's face. Clint had the feeling he had walked in on something.

"I was just telling Clint that he should stay in Glitter Gulch awhile."

"We were also talking about who came up with the idea for this kind of entertainment," Clint said.

"It doesn't really matter," Dorsett said, before April could say anything. "What matters is that it works, and the town is benefitting from it. Do you gamble, Clint?"

"Some," Clint said.

"What game?"

"Poker."

"Is that all?"

"Anything with cards," Clint said, "but I prefer poker."

"Maybe we can get up a game later. You could meet some of the other businessmen in town."

"That would be interesting."

"You don't know them," April said.

"April." Dorsett's tone was impatient. She looked at him and he said, "Just eat, don't talk."

She stared at him for a few moments, looked at Clint, then gave her attention back to her plate.

TEN

Dorsett did most of the talking during dinner, singing the praises of Glitter Gulch and—oh, by the way—of himself. Clint watched April throughout the meal and was convinced that if the girl could have gotten up and walked out she would have. Dorsett had some kind of a hold on her. Clint wondered about the other girls. Were they just working for Dorsett, or did he have a hold over them, too?

During dinner the girls who had "danced" on-stage came out and began to mingle with the customers. Clint was surprised at the way they dressed. Rather than the usual revealing dresses that saloon girls wore, they were all wearing clothing that covered them virtually from head to toe. In some cases the clothing was rather tight, but it still showed very little skin.

"What did you think of the steak?" Dorsett

asked after Holly had cleared away the plates. April's had been more than half filled when it was taken away.

"It was excellent, as promised."

"And the coffee is even better."

"Coffee sounds like a good idea."

"And then maybe we can do something about that poker game."

"Oh, I don't think I'm up for that tonight," Clint said.

"Maybe tomorrow then?" Dorsett asked.

"If I'm still in town."

"Oh, I thought I'd talked you into staying awhile."

"Let's just say I'm still thinking about it."

Dorsett had Holly bring a pot of coffee and two cups. April preferred hot tea.

One of the girls came by the table and smiled at Leo Dorsett.

"Hello, Gladys," Dorsett said.

"Mr. Dorsett. How did I do?"

Dorsett looked at Clint.

"I think I'll let Mr. Adams answer that, Gladys. What did you think of her performance, Clint?"

Clint looked up at the woman and saw that she was the blonde who had mesmerized her audience with her dancing, as well as her body.

"I think you were magnificent," he told her truthfully.

She looked pleased.

"Oh, thank you, Mr. Adams."

"I think you were great, too, Gladys."

"Thank you, Mr. Dorsett."

"Go ahead and mingle now."

"Yes, sir."

She gave Dorsett a flirty look, then graced Clint with a quick one before walking away.

"She's new," Dorsett said. "First night."

"She did very well," Clint said. Then, looking at Dorsett, he added, "Didn't she?"

"Did she, April?" Dorsett didn't seem to want to answer questions himself.

"She did fine," April said.

Dorsett was about to speak again when there was some commotion at one of the roulette tables.

"Excuse me," Dorsett said. He stood up and strode to the table. Clint watched as Dorsett imposed himself between the two men who were arguing. Without laying a hand on them he managed to dissuade them from continuing their dispute in his place. He proceeded to walk them to the front door, then stopped at the bar before returning to the table.

"That was impressive," Clint said.

"Do you think so?" April asked.

He looked at her.

"Don't you?"

"I stopped being impressed with Leo Dorsett a long time ago, Mr. Adams."

"Clint."

She didn't say anything.

"You don't like working for him?"

"I didn't say that."

"I heard what you said, April," Clint said, "what did you mean?"

"Quiet," she said, looking past him. Clint assumed this meant that Dorsett was returning to the table.

"Sorry," Dorsett said. "I don't like customers breaking up the place."

"What did you say to them?" Clint asked.

"I just told them that it would be better for everyone if they took their dispute outside."

"That was it?"

Dorsett smiled.

"I was rather emphatic."

"Don't you have anyone working for you who can do that?"

"Of course I do," Dorsett said. "I just prefer to keep my hand in . . . why? Are you looking for a job?"

"No," Clint said, "I'm not."

"Too bad," Dorsett said. "I'd love to have the Gunsmith working for me. It might even bring in more business."

Clint laughed.

"I don't think I could do better for you than the girls you had up on the stage tonight, Mr. Dorsett," Clint said, "or better than Miss Donovan, for that matter."

"Just call her April," Dorsett said, "and call me Leo. I want us to be friends, Clint."

Clint smiled and said that was nice, but the look on April's face was saying something totally different.

ELEVEN

After coffee Clint announced that he was going to turn in.

"It's still early," Dorsett argued.

"Not for me," Clint said. "I was in the saddle today. I'm just about done."

"All right then. How about if one of the girls goes back to your room with you?"

"I don't think so."

"How about Gladys?"

"Gladys is beautiful, Leo," Clint said, standing up, "but I prefer to choose my own women."

"I can't say that I blame you for that," Dorsett said, also standing. "I feel the same way."

"Seems to me you chose pretty well," Clint said.

April looked up at him with a new expression, and then smiled.

"Good night, April."

"Good night, Clint."

Dorsett studied the two of them, aware that something had just happened, but he wasn't sure what.

"Good night, Leo," Clint said.

"Good night, Clint. Come back around tomorrow. I like talking to you."

"I might do that."

"I'll try to arrange that poker game."

"I'll try and be a little more alert."

"A good night's sleep will do you good."

"It always does," Clint said.

He turned and left without looking back. As he walked back to the hotel he found that he was curious about Glitter Gulch. He could hear the sounds of voices and music coming from several other saloons, and he was curious about the quality of their "entertainment." He only had Dorsett's word that it wouldn't match the quality of The Dream Palace.

As he reached his hotel he also admitted that he was curious about April Donovan. He wondered what the chances were that he could have a conversation with her without Dorsett around.

Dorsett sat back down and looked at April.

"What do you think of our new friend?" he asked.

"If he's your new friend that gives you one, doesn't it?"

"You're pushing your luck tonight, April," Dorsett said warningly. "Why is that?"

"I don't know." She looked away. "Maybe I'm feeling self-destructive."

"Well don't," Dorsett said. "It's not good for you."

She looked at him but only for a second before averting her eyes again.

"What happened to Elsa? She didn't come out here with the rest of the girls."

"She was nervous."

"About what?" Dorsett frowned. "She didn't seem to have any trouble taking off her clothes this afternoon, or this evening."

April shrugged.

"She was nervous about coming out here with all these men."

"Well, you go back and tell her that it's part of the job. If she doesn't come out, I'm going to have to go back and get her."

"There are enough girls out here, Leo. Why don't you leave her—"

"I like my employees to do what they're paid to do, April," Dorsett said, cutting her off. "Now go and get her to do what she's paid to do—that's what I pay *you* for."

April hesitated just a moment, but that was all the resistance she could muster.

"All right," she said, standing up, "I'm going."

"And while you're back there," Dorsett said, "readjust your attitude. I'm not going to like looking at you if you're going to be frowning all the time. Understand?"

"Sure, Leo," she said. "I understand."

"There's a good girl, April."

Dorsett watched April walk across the room to a door in the back and go through. He shook his head. Maybe she wasn't going to be able to adjust her attitude herself. Maybe he was going to have to do it for her.

"All alone?" a voice asked.

He looked up and saw Gladys standing there, smiling.

"Not anymore," he said.

TWELVE

"What's the problem, Elsa?" April asked the pretty black girl.

The girl looked down at the floor. She was wearing a blue dress that went very well with her skin tone.

"Elsa?"

"I cain't go out theah, ma'am."

"Why not?"

"I's too nervous."

"But you took off your clothes, Elsa," April said. "Why didn't that make you nervous?"

" 'Cause I was up there alone, ma'am. I's nervous around people—'specially men."

"Elsa, going out there is part of your job. You knew that, didn't you?"

"Yes, ma'am."

"Mr. Dorsett's going to be real upset if you don't do it."

"I know."

"He'll want me to fire you."

The girl looked at her now with frightened eyes.

"I needs this job, ma'am. You cain't fire me."

"It's not up to me, Elsa. I'm going to leave you alone for a few minutes, but after that you better come outside. Understand?"

"Yes, ma'am, I understands."

"Good."

April patted the young woman on the shoulder and went back into the saloon. When she closed the door behind her, she looked over at the table where Dorsett was and saw Gladys sitting in the seat she'd just vacated. She felt a spark of jealousy, but then shrugged it off. If Dorsett took a liking to Gladys and made her his "main girl," maybe he'd let April leave. April decided not to interrupt them. This was one chance for her to get out.

And maybe Clint Adams was another.

Clint had removed his boots and shirt and was reclining on the bed when the knock came at the door. He was thinking things over, wondering if he should leave in the morning or stay another day. The knock was tentative, almost as if the person knocking really didn't want to be heard. He had hung his gun belt on the bedpost and now he removed the gun and carried it with him to the door.

"Who is it?"

"I—it's April Donovan. Can I come in?"

"April—"

He opened the door, keeping the gun ready.

When he saw that she was alone, he said, "Come on in."

She slipped past him into the room and he closed the door behind her.

"What are you doing here?" he asked. "Did Dorsett send you? Did he think I would prefer you to Gladys?"

"And wouldn't you?"

"Truthfully?"

"If you told me the truth," she said, "it would be a novelty."

"The truth then," he said. "Yes, I would prefer you to Gladys."

"Well then, I hate to disappoint you," she said, "but Leo didn't send me. In fact, if he knew I was here he would kill us both."

"Why?"

"Because I'm his property—that is, unless he changes his mind."

"Is there much chance of that?"

"Gladys is trying her best to convince him, even now," April said.

"I don't think she'll succeed."

"Why not?"

"Because I don't think he's a stupid man," Clint said. "Only a stupid man would trade you for her."

"Well," April said, "he's not stupid. He's cruel, brutal, and cunning."

"What did you come up here to tell me, April?"

"I'm not sure, Clint. When I saw you walk into the saloon I thought you looked like an interesting man. When you came to the table I thought Leo was buying you, like he buys everyone else."

"I can't be bought."

"I realized that after a while."

"Sit down, April."

"Do you really need that gun?"

Clint looked down at the gun in his hand, as if he'd forgotten it was there. He walked to the bedpost and holstered it.

She started to sit in the wooden chair in the room but he said, "No, on the bed. You'll be more comfortable."

"And where are you going to sit?"

He smiled, and sat down in the chair.

"You're not a very smart girl, Gladys."

Dorsett expected the girl to be insulted, but she was not. She smiled.

"I know that."

"Do you?"

"Oh, yes. Men are much smarter than I am."

Dorsett studied her. Maybe she wasn't as dumb as she made out.

He looked around, didn't see April or Elsa.

"Looking for Miss Donovan?" Gladys asked.

"Yes," he said.

"Bored with me?"

He looked at her.

"Gladys, do you know where my room is?"

"Yes, I do, Mr. Dorsett."

"Why don't you go up there and wait for me?" he suggested. "In a little while we'll see if I get bored with you."

"When will you come up?"

"I said in a little while."

"What happens if I fall asleep?"

"I'll wake you up."

"But—"

"Just go, Gladys."

"All right." Her tone was contrite. She stood up and walked to the stairs. He watched her big behind as she went up the steps, as did every other man in the place.

At some other time he would have run right up there after her, but at the moment—and since that afternoon, actually—he was more interested in the black girl, Elsa. April was supposed to have gotten her to mingle, and now there was no sign of her or the black girl.

He stood up and went to look for Elsa himself.

THIRTEEN

"I was hired as one of his girls, but he soon realized how smart I was."

"How smart are you?" Clint asked.

"Very smart," April told him.

"Then what are you doing with him?"

"I thought it was the smart thing to do."

"And it wasn't?"

"It was, for a while—for a very little while it was actually good for both of us. He won't admit this, but the girls taking off their clothes? It was my idea."

"Is that so?"

"Yes, it is. When the other places in town found out we were doing it, they started, too."

"How did you come up with the idea?"

"I met a girl, a French girl, in San Francisco, and she told me about it."

"And you told Dorsett?"

"That's right. After that all we had to do was find girls who would do it."

"And was that hard?"

She laughed.

"Not at all. There were plenty of them willing to do it."

"What about you?"

"That's what Leo asked me."

"Sorry."

"That's all right. It's a legitimate question. I'd do it if I needed the money. Leo pays me enough to manage the girls."

"So what's the problem?"

"It's the other things he does."

"Like what?"

"Sex, for one."

"He forces you to have sex with him?"

"Yes."

"Did you ever do it willingly?"

"Yes," she said, looking away, "in the beginning."

"What happened?"

"His cruel side came out. I wanted us to have a strictly business relationship, but he didn't agree. He . . . uses force to get what he wants."

"He beat you?"

"He has," she said, "on occasion, but more often than not he uses the same method you saw him use tonight—intimidation."

"Why don't you leave?"

"He wouldn't let me go."

"Have you tried?"

"No."

"Why not?"

"I'm afraid of him." She looked at Clint then. "There are only two ways I can leave him."

"What are they?"

"First, if he lets me leave."

"And second?"

"If I get someone to help me."

When Dorsett appeared, Elsa looked up.

"Mistuh Dorsett."

"What are you doing back here, Elsa?" he asked.

"I—"

"You're supposed to be outside, with the other girls."

"I cain't, Mistuh Dorsett—"

"Why not, Elsa?"

"I's nervous."

"About what?"

"A-about men."

"Elsa," Dorsett asked, "have you ever been with a man before?"

She looked down at the floor.

"No."

Dorsett stared down at her. She was a virgin! He was suddenly very excited. He had a raging erection.

"Elsa," he said, "come with me."

"Mistuh Dorsett," she said, "I think I made a mistake comin' to work for you—"

"I don't think so, Elsa," Dorsett said. He was aware that his mouth was dry. "You danced very well out there."

"Thank you."

"The men liked you very much."

She ducked her head.

"Come with me."

"Where?"

"I'm going to teach you something."

"What?"

Dorsett was tired of asking nicely. He reached down, grasped her wrist, and pulled her to her feet.

"Ow," she cried out, "you're hurting me."

"Come with me—now!"

He pulled her to the back stairway and up to the second floor. She tried to resist, but he was too strong for her. At one point she began to yell, but he turned and slapped her. More than hurting her, it stunned her into silence.

He had opened the door to his room and pushed her inside before he remembered that Gladys was there. The blonde was on his bed, naked.

"Oh goody," she said, clapping her hands, "more company."

FOURTEEN

"You want me to help you?"

"It's silly, I know," April said. "We've only just met. Why should you help me?"

Clint stared at her for a few moments.

"When's the last time he beat you?" he asked finally.

"Not for a while," she said, "but he bruised me yesterday."

"Where?"

She hesitated, then stood up and undid the back of her dress. She slid it off her shoulders just far enough to show the black-and-blue marks on her smooth skin.

"How did he do that?"

"Why do you want to know?"

"Just humor me."

She pulled her dress back up, but didn't close it in the back.

"He was forcing me to do things to him—you know, with my mouth."

Clint could envision her on her knees in front of Dorsett, he with his hands on her shoulders, hurting her.

"How can I help?"

"Can't I do more than watch?" Gladys asked.

"Just make sure she does it right," Dorsett told her.

"It would be easier if I showed her."

"All right," Dorsett said, "show her."

Both women were naked and on their knees in front of him. The blonde was willing—more than willing—and the black girl was not.

Dorsett was naked, and erect.

"Show her."

"Watch me," Gladys said to Elsa.

She took hold of Dorsett's penis at the base, opened her mouth, and took him inside. She began to suck him, slowly working her way up and down the length of him.

"Jesus . . ." Dorsett said. She was damned good. "That's enough . . . that's enough!"

He pushed her away.

"Let her do it."

"Go ahead, sweetie," Gladys said. "It's real tasty."

"I cain't," Elsa said, looking at Dorsett's erect penis with wide eyes. "It's too big!"

"No, it ain't," Gladys said. "It'll fit just fine."

"Come on, Elsa," Dorsett said, "do it!"

He watched her as she opened her mouth, closed her eyes, and took him inside. Her mouth was wet and hot as she began to suck him.

"Good," Dorsett said, "good, that's good . . ."

"Easy, sweetie," Gladys said, "go easy . . ."

Jesus, Dorsett thought, Gladys was good, but this girl was so young, and so innocent . . . a virgin with his penis in her mouth.

Before he knew it he exploded into her mouth, and she began to gag and choke. She tried to get away, but he held her with both hands, kept her mouth on him, until in her panic to get away from him she bit him!

"Damn it!" he said, and punched her.

"Take me with you when you leave," April said.

"Just like that?"

"Just like that," she said.

"Won't he come after you?"

"After *me*, yes," she said, "but maybe he won't come after you."

"Why not?"

"You're the Gunsmith."

"I didn't get the impression that would stop him," Clint said. "How many men does he have working for him?"

She shrugged.

"Maybe half a dozen."

"I wouldn't want to go up against six men, April."

"Then what can I do?"

"We'll go and talk to him," Clint said. "Maybe I can get him to let you go."

"How?"

"I don't know how," he said. "We'll just have to see what happens."

"When can we do this?" she asked, sounding like a little girl.

"It's late now," Clint said. "Why don't we do it tomorrow?"

"All right."

She made no move to get up off the bed.

"April . . ."

"Can I stay here tonight?"

He stared at her.

"You don't have to."

She smiled.

"I know I don't," she said. "I don't want to go back to him and have to try to tell him where I've been."

"All right," he said. "Stay here . . . but you don't have to do anything you don't want to do."

"I know that, Clint," she said. "I know that, and I appreciate it. I haven't been given a choice like that in a long time."

And with that free choice she stood up and let her dress fall to the floor.

FIFTEEN

"I haven't made love this way in a long time," April said a short time later.

"What way is that?"

She snuggled up against him and said, "Willingly."

"I can't imagine forcing a woman to have sex with me," he said, shaking his head.

"That's because you're a decent man," she said. "Believe me, a decent man is a hard thing to find."

He slid his arm around her and held her tightly.

"Can I ask you a question?" she asked.

"Of course."

"Why would you go up against Dorsett for me? Is it because I slept with you?"

"I told you before you didn't have to do this."

"Please, don't be upset with me."

"I'm not."

"I'm just trying to understand this," she said.

"I'm used to men wanting something from me before they'll give anything back. I guess I just don't
understand you."

"You said I was a decent man."

"I guess you are," she said. "To tell you the
truth, I don't think I've ever known one before, so
how would I recognize it?"

"Well, there are a lot of them out there, April,
believe me."

"Well," she said, sliding her hand down over his
belly, "if I died tonight I'd be happy that I met at
least one."

Her hand touched his penis, which reacted immediately. As he came erect she stroked him with
her fingertips, spending extra time on the under-
side.

He returned the favor by moving his hand over
her smooth belly until he found her with his fingers. As he touched her she became moist. With
the tip of his middle finger he found her clit and
encircled it. She gasped and fell onto her back, her
eyes closed and her legs wide. He didn't mind that
she had stopped touching him. He was intent on
giving April Donovan as much pleasure as he
could. She was beautiful, physically very sensi-
tive, and she had been having forced sex for a long
time. He doubted that Leo Dorsett ever had her
pleasure in mind when they were together.

Clint removed his hand from her and pulled the
sheet down to expose her body. He spent a lot of
time running his hands over her, touching her
breasts, her nipples, touching her flesh everywhere he could touch it before going back to her
moist vagina. He slid his middle finger over her,

teasing her until her body tensed and arched when he once again touched her clit.

"Oh, Jesus . . ." she said, staring at the ceiling with wide eyes. "Nobody has *ever* taken this much time . . ."

"You're a beautiful woman, April," Clint told her, continuing to stroke her, "you deserve to have a lot of time spent on you."

"Oh . . ." she said, unable to form any other kind of answer.

While he continued to manipulate her with his hand, he leaned over and began to kiss her nipples. He circled them with his tongue, then sucked on them. He kissed lower then, running his mouth over her ribs, her belly, touching her navel with the tip of his tongue, working lower still until he was nestled between her legs, until his cheeks were wet from her, his tongue lapping at her, bringing her body more and more taut until he thought she might snap—and then she did. She cried out and began to buck beneath him. He held her fast, his elbows pinning her thighs to the bed, keeping his mouth in contact with her.

She reached down, either to push him away or hold him closer, but she was so frantic that her hands flailed away harmlessly.

Finally he released her, mounted her, and entered her in one swift motion. She gasped and closed her arms and legs around him, holding him tightly.

He slid his hands beneath her buttocks, held her tightly, and they moved together that way for a long time. . . .

SIXTEEN

When they woke in the morning, April was a little tentative. Clint would have liked to have made love again, but he didn't press it. He could see that she was nervous and wanted to give her time to sort things out for herself.

They got up and got dressed, and he suggested that they go down to the hotel dining room for some breakfast. Halfway through breakfast she still hadn't said much, and he decided to try to get her to open up.

"April? Do you want to talk?"

"About what?"

"About anything."

"What's there to talk about? Nothing's going to change."

"Why not?"

She looked at him and asked, "Do you still want to help me?"

"Well, sure," Clint said, "why would that change?"

"Well, I thought . . ."

"You thought once you'd had sex with me that I'd forget my promise?"

"Every other man has."

"Well, I won't," Clint said. "I told you I would try to help you, and I will."

She sat back and stared at him, heaving a sigh of relief.

"I'm sorry," she said, "I just thought—"

"Never mind what you thought," Clint said. "Finish your breakfast and we'll go and have a talk with Leo."

She sat forward and attacked the second half of her breakfast with much more vigor than the first.

"Leo is not just going to let me go, you know," she said. "Not without a fight."

"We'll see about that," Clint said. "If we can get you away from him without a fight, I'd like to do it that way."

"And if not?"

"Like I said, let's wait and see."

As they left the hotel, Clint asked April, "Will Leo be up this early?"

"That depends on what he was doing last night."

"I thought you were his woman."

"That never stopped him from taking any of the others to bed," she said, and then added, "sometimes more than one at a time."

Clint looked at her.

"Yes," she said, looking away, "I've been involved in some of those nights. I've been to bed with lots of men, Clint, but Leo Dorsett is the sickest man I've ever been with. He'll try anything once, and he usually keeps on going."

As they approached The Dream Palace they noticed a crowd of people out front.

"What's going on?" April wondered aloud.

"I don't know," Clint said. "Let's find out."

It was just after nine a.m. and Clint was surprised to see the front door of the place open. People were crowding around, trying to get a look inside. Clint pushed his way past, with April right behind him.

Inside they saw several men standing around, and Clint noticed they were all wearing deputy's badges.

"Can't come in here," one man said to Clint, then noticed April. "Oh, it's you, Miss Donovan. The sheriff's been looking for you."

"Why?"

"I'll let him tell you that. Wait here." The deputy, a man in his forties, turned to one of the other, younger men and said, "Don't let them leave."

The man nodded and fixed Clint with a hard look.

"Boo," Clint said, but the man didn't flinch.

The first deputy went upstairs and reappeared moments later with Sheriff Sam Osborne. The lawman looked grim.

"Miss Donovan," the man said. "Mr Adams."

"Sheriff, what's going on?" April asked.

"Miss Donovan, would you mind telling me where you've been all night?"

She looked at Clint, who nodded.

"I've been with Mr. Adams, in his hotel."

"Did Mr. Dorsett send you over there?"

"No, he didn't," she said. "I went on my own."

"How well do you know Mr. Adams?"

"We met yesterday."

"What time were you with him from?"

"I went to his hotel around ten, and I was there the whole night."

"And he never left the room?"

"No."

"What about her?" Osborne asked Clint.

"Never left the room," Clint said, "or the bed."

"Hmm," Osborne said, giving both of them a suspicious stare.

"Can you tell us what's going on, Sheriff?" Clint asked.

"One of the girls who works in this place turned up dead this morning."

"Oh, God," April said, covering her mouth. "Who was it?"

"I don't know her name," Osborne said. "A little black girl."

"Oh, no," April said, "Elsa." She looked at Clint. "I told you about her last night."

"The nervous girl?"

She nodded.

"How was she killed?" Clint asked.

"She was beaten to death."

"Oh, my God," April said. "I have to go up—"

"I don't think you want to see her, Miss Donovan," Osborne said.

"But—"

"I think he's right, April," Clint said. "Don't go up there."

"I'm going to ask the two of you to accompany Deputy Simson over to my office."

Simson was apparently the deputy who had gone to fetch the sheriff upstairs.

"What for?" Clint asked.

"I've got some more questions to ask after I finish here."

"About what?"

"I'll ask them in my office, Mr. Adams."

"Are we under arrest?"

Osborne fixed Clint with a level stare.

"If you were under arrest," he said, "I'd have your gun by now, wouldn't I?"

Clint backed off.

"I guess so."

"I'm asking you to do me a favor and go to my office with the deputy. Can you do that?"

"Sure," Clint said. "Come on, April."

"Who killed her?" April asked Osborne. "Who did it?"

Osborne looked at her and said, "That's what I'm going to try and find out, Miss Donovan."

SEVENTEEN

Clint and April walked over to the sheriff's office with Deputy Simson. While sitting there they tried to get more information from him, but he either didn't know anything or wasn't talking.

"Stop asking me questions," Simson said. "I ain't gonna tell you nothin'."

"You're not, can't, or won't?" Clint asked.

"Don't make a difference," Simson said. "I ain't talkin' to you, so just shut up—excuse me, ma'am."

"Forget it, Frank."

Clint wasn't surprised that April knew the deputy by his first name. The man was probably a regular customer at The Dream Palace.

Clint leaned over to April while the deputy was pouring himself a cup of coffee from a pot atop a potbellied stove.

"Has the sheriff ever been to Leo's place?"

"He's been there," she said, "but not usually to see the show."

"Then why?"

"To pick up his money."

"You mean Sheriff Osborne takes payoffs?"

April nodded.

"From all of the saloons and businesses in town."

"What are you talkin' about now?" the deputy asked.

"Miss Donovan was just telling me about the sheriff, Deputy."

"What about him? He's a good lawman, always has been. What's wrong with that?"

"There's nothing wrong with it."

"Then shut up about it—excuse me—"

"Oh, never mind, Frank. How long are you going to keep us here?"

"Until the sheriff gets here, Miss Donovan. There's nothing else I can do. I have to follow my orders."

"Of course you do. Frank, could we have some of that coffee?"

Frank frowned.

"I'll have to look around for some cups."

He did and found two. April poured a cup of coffee for herself and Clint, and while they were drinking it the door opened and Sheriff Osborne walked in. He looked annoyed, went directly to the coffeepot, and picked it up. When he found it was empty he became *really* annoyed. He turned and glared at his deputy.

"The coffeepot's empty."

"Uh—"

"How many times have I told you not to take the last cup of coffee without making another pot."

"I didn't know—"

"You couldn't feel that the pot was empty?"

"I didn't pour, Sheriff," Simson said, "it was Miss Donovan."

Osborne looked over at Clint and April and saw the cups in their hands.

"Sorry we took the last of your coffee, Sheriff," Clint said. "We didn't know how long we'd have to wait for you."

"Frank was nice enough to find us cups," April said.

"Frank's a real nice fella," Osborne said. He put the empty pot down and glared at Simson. "Would you mind making some more coffee?"

"Uh, sure, Sheriff."

Simson hurried out of Osborne's chair so the sheriff could sit behind his own desk.

"What's going on, Sheriff?" Clint asked.

"Where is Elsa?" April asked.

Osborne looked at April and answered her first.

"The girl is over at the undertaker's, Miss Donovan."

"Did you find out who killed her?"

"Not yet."

"I don't understand how this could have happened," April said, shaking her head.

"What's to understand, Miss Donovan? She went upstairs with the wrong man."

"That's just it," April said. "She was a new girl. She just started last night."

"So?"

"So she was too nervous to even go out and mingle with the customers," April said. "I don't think she could have gone upstairs with a man."

"Well, she did," Osborne said.

"With who?" Clint asked.

"We don't know. I've got to question the other women about that, but they were too upset for me to talk to this morning."

"What did Mr. Dorsett say?" April asked. "Did he see who she went upstairs with?"

"No."

"Why not? Wasn't he watching?"

"No," Osborne said, "he wasn't. He was, uh, upstairs himself."

April hesitated a moment, then said, "Oh."

"Mr. Dorsett also said he didn't see you around last night, Miss Donovan, or you, Mr. Adams."

"I said good night to Mr. Dorsett early and went to my hotel, Sheriff," Clint said. "That's why he didn't see me around."

"I left the saloon soon after," April said. "I didn't go back."

Osborne looked at her.

"Not until this morning?"

"That's right."

"And you were with Mr. Adams all night?"

"That's right."

"Do you suspect one of us of this killing?" Clint asked. He knew that if one of them was suspected, it was going to be him.

"I'm just asking questions, Mr. Adams, and to tell you the truth, I'm no detective. I'm not comfortable with this thing."

"What are you going to do?"

"Oh, I'm still going to do my job," Osborne said. "But I think there's a good chance that the man who did this has left town already."

"I told you," April said, "she wouldn't have gone upstairs with a man."

Osborne ignored her.

"I'd like you to stay around town, though," Osborne said to Clint. "That is, until I'm sure."

"Sure that the man who did it is gone, or sure that I didn't do it?"

"Just don't leave town until I tell you to, Mr. Adams," Osborne said, "and I'll be happy. Understand?"

"Sure," Clint said, "I understand, Sheriff. Can we go now?"

"Sure," Osborne said, "you can go. I'll find you if I think of any other questions."

Clint and April got up and walked to the door. April had put her coffee cup down on the desk. Clint's was still in his hand.

"Mr. Adams."

Clint turned.

"Yes?"

"You have my coffee cup."

Clint frowned, not sure he'd heard him right, then looked down at the cup in his hand.

"Oh, sorry." He walked to the desk and put it down. "Sorry," he said again.

Clint and April left. Osborne leaned forward, picked up his cup, and cleaned it with a bandanna. He swiveled his chair around and looked at Simson.

"Is that coffee ready yet?" he bellowed.

EIGHTEEN

Outside April turned to Clint.

"It's horrible about Elsa. Clint, I swear that girl would not have gone upstairs with a man. Not last night."

"Then who do you think killed her?"

"I don't know."

"Do you want to find out?"

"Well, of course. Why do you ask?"

"We were going to try and get you out of here, remember?"

"Oh, yes, of course I remember. But the sheriff just told you that you couldn't leave town."

"That's right."

"So we might as well wait before talking to Leo about that."

"And talk to him about murder, instead?"

Her eyes widened.

"You think Leo killed her?"

"Is he capable of that?"

She hesitated only a moment, then said, "Well . . . yes. He is basically a violent man."

Clint frowned. That was not in keeping with what he had seen last night in the saloon. Dorsett had broken up that fight without taking any physical action at all.

"I know what you're thinking."

"Do you?"

"Yes. There's something you should know about Leo Dorsett's violence."

"What's that?"

"It's usually directed at women."

Clint stared at April and realized that she would know that better than anyone.

"What do you want to do, April?"

"I want to go and see Elsa's body."

"Why?"

"I hired her, Clint," April said. "She was a sweet kid, and she's dead because I hired her."

"You can't blame yourself for that."

"I want to see her."

"Okay," Clint said, "we'll go to the undertaker's office."

"After that I want to talk to the other girls," April said. "One of them must have seen something last night. Will you come with me?"

"Sure, I'll come."

"I'm real glad you're here, Clint," she said. "Real glad."

NINETEEN

As Clint walked April down the street toward the undertaker's office, Leo Dorsett watched them from the window of his room. Dorsett had been wondering where April had spent the night. Now he knew. It was his own fault, really, for bringing Adams to their table last night, but he'd been impressed with Adams even before he found out who he really was.

He had to put that aside now, though. Clint Adams or not, Dorsett had to worry about himself—especially after what had happened last night.

He wanted to talk to April, but knew he'd have to do that away from Adams. The two of them looked pretty close down there on the street after only one night together. If Clint Adams had treated her right last night, Dorsett knew that April would follow the man anywhere. Dorsett hated the thought of losing April. He wasn't finished with her, and she knew how to handle the girls.

He also didn't like the idea of a woman leaving him of her own volition. Gunsmith or not, it was not going to be that easy for April Donovan to leave him, or Glitter Gulch.

He turned and went to his closet. While he slipped into his shoulder rig and jacket he thought about Gladys. He still wasn't sure just how smart—or dumb—the woman was, and it was important for him to find out.

He left his room, went downstairs, and walked over to Jake, the bartender, who was setting up the bar.

"Bad break about Elsa, Boss," Jake said.

"Yeah. Have you seen Pullman?"

"Not this morning."

"Find him, tell him I want him."

"I got to set up the bar, Boss—"

"Then have someone find him, but make it fast. I'll be in my office."

"Okay, Boss. Are we openin' regular today?"

"We open every day regular, don't we, Jake?"

"Uh, I just thought, what with that girl bein' killed—"

"What did you see last night, Jake?"

"Uh, what do ya mean?"

"Just what I asked you," Dorsett said. "What did you see?"

Jake hesitated, then said, "Boss, I didn't see nothin'."

Dorsett studied the fat man for a few moments, then said, "Okay, Jake. Get me Pullman, will you?"

"Sure, Boss, sure."

Dorsett went to his office to await the appearance of Jim Pullman. Pullman was his right hand, in charge of the other men who worked for him. He kept about half a dozen men on his payroll, but he had enough money to hire more when the need arose.

Clint Adams just might qualify as a need.

TWENTY

Clint went into the back room with April, where the undertaker had laid out Elsa's body.

"Are you sure about this?" he asked her before they went in.

"I'm sure."

They stared at her body now. Her face had been severely beaten, her lips split and teeth broken, her body badly bruised.

"God," April said.

"Come on, April," Clint said. "You don't need to look at this any longer than necessary."

She allowed him to turn her and walk her out into the other room. The undertaker, a man named Wallace, was waiting there.

"Who is going to pay for the burial, please?" he asked.

April looked at Clint.

"Mr. Dorsett is going to pay," Clint said. "The

young lady worked for him."

"Excellent."

"Let's go," Clint said to April. He physically steered her out the door.

"I have to talk to the other girls," April said, "and to Leo."

"Why Leo?"

"He knows something."

"Why do you say that?"

"Because Leo knows everything that goes on in his place," April said. "That's why I can't understand how this could have happened."

"What do you mean?"

"Elsa could not have gotten that beaten up without some noise," April said. "She would have screamed, people would have heard the commotion. Leo would have known something was wrong, and he would have stopped it."

"But he didn't."

"Right."

"So you think he did it?"

"I don't know," she said. "You asked me before if I thought he was capable. He is. But I don't know . . ."

"Well," Clint said, "we'll ask him, but first I want you to calm down a bit."

"I am calm."

"Let's go back to the room," Clint said. "I want you to lie down for a while."

"What are you going to do?"

"I think maybe I ought to have another talk with the sheriff."

"About what?"

"Oh . . . things."

They were walking back to the hotel.

"What kind of things?"

"His deputies, for one. Where were they when all of this was happening? I'd also like to find out about his money arrangements with the merchants here in town."

"You're going to ask him about his payoffs?"

"Not exactly."

When they reached the hotel he stopped.

"Wait in the room. I'll be back in a little while."

"When?"

"In a while. Just don't leave the room, okay? Tell the clerk to give you the key."

"Be careful," April said. "Be very careful. Something is not right here."

"I'm always careful."

"Watch out for a big man with a scar under his left eye," she said.

"Who's that?"

"His name's Pullman. He works for Leo."

"Pullman."

She nodded.

"I'll remember. Go upstairs now, April. Go ahead."

April went inside and Clint turned and walked back toward the sheriff's office.

TWENTY-ONE

Sam Osborne looked up from his desk as the door to his office opened. He was surprised to see Clint Adams come walking in.

"Something else I can do for you?"

"Yeah," Clint said. He looked around and saw that they were alone. On a table next to the potbellied stove were the other two coffee cups. Osborne was still working on his.

"You mind?" Clint asked.

"Help yourself."

Clint walked to the coffeepot and poured himself a cup, then walked back in front of the sheriff's desk and sat down.

"I thought I told you I'd find you when I thought of some more questions."

"It just so happens that I've thought of some questions, Sheriff."

"Is that a fact? Like what, for instance?"

"Like where were your deputies when that girl was being killed last night?"

"I was on duty alone last night, if it's any of your business, Adams," Osborne said. "What my deputies do in their off time is their business."

"Did you question Leo Dorsett about the girl?"

"Of course I did. She died in his house, didn't she? She worked for him."

"What did he have to say?"

Osborne looked at the ceiling and said, "I don't even know why I'm answering these questions."

"Maybe it's because you don't have a clue how to go about finding the killer of that girl."

Osborne glared at Clint and for a moment it looked as if he was going to protest. Instead he stood up, got himself some more coffee, and then sat down.

"You're right, of course," he said, passing a weary hand over his face. "I've been a lawman most of my life, Adams, but I have never been a detective."

"Then maybe you need a little help."

"From you?"

"Do you have any other choices?"

"There's one problem."

"What's that?"

"You're a stranger in town."

"What's that mean?"

"It means I have to suspect you."

"I didn't kill that girl, Sheriff," Clint said. "If I did, then you have to call April a liar."

"Maybe you both did it."

"Why would we?"

"I don't know, Adams," Osborne said. "Why

would anyone do that to a woman?"

"I saw the body, Sheriff," Clint said. "It looks to me like someone acted out of anger."

Osborne stared off into space for a moment and then said, "I've seen a lot of things in my life, Adams, but I haven't seen that many women beaten to death."

Clint studied the man and came to the conclusion that the sheriff was serious. Could Leo Dorsett pay this man to look the other way?

"I have a suggestion," Clint said.

"What's that?"

"First, you have to forget about me as a suspect. I didn't even know the woman."

"And if I do that?"

"I think April Donovan and I could get more out of the other women than you could. Let April talk to them about what happened last night."

"Miss Donovan . . . and you?"

"I'll be with her."

Osborne frowned.

"Are you going to take on Leo Dorsett, Adams?"

"That depends on what you mean by taking him on."

"Leo Dorsett doesn't like anyone playing with his women," Osborne said. "Not unless you're paying for the pleasure."

"Well, I'm not."

"Playing?"

"Paying."

"What's goin' on between you and Miss Donovan?"

"That's like me asking you if you're taking money from the merchants in town."

Osborne's eyes flashed.

"That's none of your business!"

Clint smiled.

"That's what I mean."

Osborne glared at Clint for a few moments, then looked away. At that moment Clint was convinced that April had been telling the truth about Osborne. The lawman was obviously taking pay-offs from the merchants in Glitter Gulch.

"I take your point," Osborne said. "All right, why don't you and Miss Donovan talk to the girls."

"Fine."

Clint stood up.

"Of course you'll let me know what you find out."

"You'll be the first," Clint assured him.

"I better be," Osborne said. "I know your reputation, Adams, and it doesn't intimidate me."

"Thanks for the coffee," Clint said and left.

TWENTY-TWO

Clint went back to the hotel and knocked on the door to his room. April didn't answer right away and for a moment he was afraid she might not be inside—then the door opened.

"You didn't ask who it was," he scolded her.

She wiped her face sleepily.

"I fell asleep waiting for you."

He closed the door.

"Look, April, Elsa's dead, and if Dorsett is as dangerous as you say, you're going to have to be more careful."

"I can solve that problem."

"How?"

She put her arms around his waist and pressed her head to his chest.

"Just stay with me at all times from now on."

He wrapped his arms around her and held her. She was smart, and he thought she was strong—

or she could be if she got away from Leo Dorsett.
Maybe all he had to do was lend her his strength
for a while.

"Okay, April," he said, "we'll try it that way for
now."

They went down to the dining room to have coffee.

"You got the sheriff to let us question the girls?"
April asked.

"Yes."

"Why would he do that?"

"Because, like he said, he's not a detective."

"Neither am I," she said. "Are you?"

"No, but I have had some experience asking
questions."

"So then *you* ask them."

"No," Clint said, "you ask the questions, I'll
just listen to the answers. Do you think the girls
will tell you the truth?"

"They will, unless they're afraid of Leo."

"So if they're lying, it will be because he's
scared them."

"Right."

"And if he's frightening the girls, it will mean
he has something to hide."

"Like he killed Elsa?"

"But why?"

"Maybe she told him no."

"Would that be reason enough for him?"

"You haven't been listening to me," she said.
"He uses violence against women. That's what he
does. It makes him feel in control, it makes him
feel like a man."

"I have an idea."

"What?"

"What if he was the one to leave Glitter Gulch, instead of you?"

"What?"

"And you became the owner."

"Well, that would sure be better all around for everyone," April said. "How do you intend to get him to do that?"

"I don't know," Clint said, "but while I'm trying to figure it out, why don't we go and talk to the girls?"

"All right."

"How many are there?"

"Eight," she said, then closed her eyes and said, "I mean, seven."

"How many new girls?"

"Two . . . Elsa was the third."

"Let's talk to the others first, the ones who know you—and who you know—better."

"They also know Leo better."

"Well," he said, standing up, "we have to start someplace."

TWENTY-THREE

"Come," Leo Dorsett called out in response to a knock on his office door.

The door opened and Jim Pullman walked in. He was a tall, dark-haired man, wide in the shoulders, deep-chested, but rangy. Dorsett had personally seen Pullman take apart as many as three men at a time, all larger than him. Pullman had a way of doing his job without building himself the kind of reputation that Clint Adams had, but that didn't make him any less capable.

"I heard you wanted to see me," Pullman said.

"Sit down."

"First," Pullman said, and walked to Dorsett's private bar. He poured himself some of Dorsett's finest brandy and then sat down. He rested the ankle of one long leg on his knee and settled back into the chair with the brandy snifter in both hands.

"What can I do for you?"

"You know who Clint Adams is?"

"Yes."

"He's the Gunsmith—"

"I said I know who he is," Pullman said.

Pullman had worked for Dorsett since he'd first opened The Dream Palace, and he had done everything he'd been asked—and paid—to do. However, he never failed to irk Dorsett with his apparent inability to call him "Mr." Dorsett. He wasn't disrespectful at any time. He never referred to Dorsett in a derogatory way, but he managed never to call him "Mr." or "sir," either of which Dorsett would have liked.

"Is he in town?"

"Yes."

"Does it look as if he's going to be a problem?"

"I had a problem last night."

"I heard. Somebody killed one of your girls. You think it was Adams?"

"I don't know who it was," Dorsett said. He stared at the glass in Pullman's hands. "Are you going to drink that?"

Pullman looked down at the brandy.

"I'm waiting for it to warm in my hands."

Dorsett didn't know what to say to that.

"What do you want me to do?"

Dorsett almost said, "What do you want me to do, *sir*?"

"I want you to be around," Dorsett said. "Somebody killed one of my girls. I want you around in case they try again."

"What makes you think they will?" Pullman asked. "What makes you think it wasn't some cowboy who's long gone?"

"I don't know," Dorsett said, "but I want you around, just in case. I also want you around in case I do have some trouble with Clint Adams."

Pullman thought that over for a few moments, then said, "That would be interesting."

"Also, keep McCarver and the others ready."

"If I need them," Pullman said, "they'll be ready."

"Pullman, I don't think you'd be foolish enough to go up against Clint Adams alone."

Pullman chose that moment to sip from his drink.

"I have another problem," Dorsett continued.

"What's that?"

"April Donovan."

"You're having a problem with your woman?"

"With my employee," Dorsett said. "I think she might be trying to leave."

"I thought you had your women under control."

"I do," Dorsett said tightly, "but I think she's planning to use Clint Adams against me."

"Do you need me for Adams or April?"

"I can handle April, Pullman."

"But not Adams."

"I could handle Adams without a gun," Dorsett said. "I need you to handle him with a gun."

Pullman finished his brandy and put the empty glass down on Dorsett's desk.

"What about the sheriff?"

"I don't think he'll be a problem."

"I mean, why don't you ask him for help? It's his job."

"I don't want him, I want you."

"Is he trying to find out who killed the girl?"

"Yes," Dorsett said, "*that's* his job. We'll let him do his, and you do yours."

Pullman nodded and stood up.

"I'll be around."

"Stay close, Pullman."

"I said I'll be around," Pullman repeated. "One thing."

"What's that?"

"If I have to face Adams, I'll expect a bonus."

"You'll get one," Dorsett said, "if you're alive to collect it."

Pullman stared at Dorsett until the other man got fidgety, then said, "Fair enough."

TWENTY-FOUR

Clint and April walked over to The Dream Palace. The front door was open but there were no customers inside yet. Jake, the fat bartender, looked up as they walked in and smiled.

"Mornin', Miss Donovan."

"Good morning, Jake."

"You missed the excitement last night."

"I guess so."

"Too bad about that girl."

"Yes, it was. Is Mr. Dorsett around?"

"He's in his office."

"And the girls?"

"They haven't come down yet."

"Okay, thanks."

"You want some coffee, Miss Donovan?"

"No, thanks, Jake."

"How about your friend?"

"No, thanks," Clint said.

"We're going upstairs, Jake. See you later."

"Sure, Miss Donovan."

They mounted the steps and were halfway up when a door in the back opened and a man stepped out. He started across the floor then stopped and looked up at them. For a moment his eyes locked with Clint's, and then he continued on and went out the door.

"That was Pullman," April said in an unsteady voice.

"I guessed," Clint said. He looked at her and smiled. "Come on. Let's go talk to the girls."

They started at the first room in the front. The girl's name was Monique.

"Her real name is Frances, but we changed it," April told Clint just before they knocked on her door.

Frances/Monique was a tall redhead with a sleek, rangy body that had almost no breasts but a beautiful butt. He had been able to see that last night.

"Good morning, April," Monique said, then looked Clint up and down. "Who's your friend?"

"My name is Clint Adams."

"Pleased to meet you, Clint."

"Monique, we'd like to ask you a few questions," April said.

"About what?"

"Can we come in?"

"Sure." She shrugged and backed up to let them enter, then closed the door. "What's this all about?"

"Elsa," April said.

"What about her? She got killed."

"Monique," April said, "did you see Elsa last night after the show?"

"Of course."

"Where?"

"Where I saw all the girls, in the back. We were dressing to come back out and mingle."

"But Elsa didn't want to come out."

Monique shrugged.

"If she didn't want to do the whole job then you should have fired her, I guess."

"But did you see her come back out last night at all?" April asked.

"Well, I didn't see her," Monique said, "but she must have come out, otherwise how would she end up in her room with a man?"

April turned and looked at Clint, who nodded, indicating that he had heard enough.

"Okay, thanks, Monique."

"Is that all?" she asked, toying with her long red hair. She was looking at Clint, not at April.

"That's all, for now," Clint said.

"Come back again," Monique said to Clint as he and April went out the door, "anytime."

They walked down the hall but stopped before they came to the next door.

"What did you think?" Clint asked.

"She's telling the truth. She didn't see Elsa on the floor last night."

"But she assumes that she was."

"Yes," April said. "She believes that some man came upstairs with Elsa and killed her."

"Whose room is this?" Clint asked.

"Alice's."

They talked to Alice, and got the same response. Alice had not seen Elsa on the floor but assumed that she was there.

Going from room to room they also got the same story from the other women.

The girls answered the door in various stages of dress and undress, and none of them appeared shy around Clint. There was one woman that Clint had not seen perform the night before. Her name was Leona. She was dark-haired and dark-eyed, and as far as Clint could see, very sexy. He wondered why she hadn't danced until he saw the reason on her thigh as she adjusted her robe. There were bruises there, ugly black, blue, and yellow bruises.

When they got outside her room Clint asked April, "Where did she get those bruises?"

"Where do you think?"

"From Dorsett?"

She nodded.

"When the girls are bruised they don't dance," April told him.

"How often does he do that?"

"Every week at least one of the girls is bruised."

"Why do they put up with it?" Clint asked.

"Because Leo pays well," April said, "and they're afraid of him."

"If they left they wouldn't have to be afraid."

"I've already told you that I'm afraid to leave on my own," she said. "They all feel the same way."

"Has any woman ever left?"

"Sure," April said, "but not on her own. Every once in a while Leo kicks one out."

"Maybe that's the answer, then."

"I don't think so. He does a lot more to them than just kick them out. It's not worth it."

"Any girls left?"

She nodded.

"Gladys, one of the new girls."

"The big blonde?"

"Yes."

"You said you saw her with Dorsett last night."

"That's right."

Clint knocked on her door and said, "This should be interesting."

TWENTY-FIVE

When Gladys opened the door she had a robe wrapped around her and her arms folded in front of her. It was a decidedly defensive posture.

"Miss Donovan," she said, but looked at Clint.

"Gladys, can we come in?"

"I'm really kind of tired, Miss Donovan."

"It won't take long, Gladys."

"Well . . . all right."

When they were inside Gladys sat on the bed, her arms still folded in front of her. Her shoulders were hunched as well. Clint was thinking he'd like to see her without the robe, and it had nothing to do with her incredible body. He wanted to know if she was bruised.

"Gladys, last night I saw you sitting with Mr. Dorsett," April said.

"He's the boss," the girl said. "He wanted me to sit with him."

"How long were you with him?"

"Just a little while."

"And then what?"

"I . . . went upstairs."

"Did you see Elsa last night?"

"Elsa?"

"The little black girl."

"Oh, her . . . she's dead . . . no, I didn't see her. I mean, I saw her on the stage, but I didn't see her after that."

"You didn't see her come out onto the floor to mingle with the customers?"

"Um, no, I didn't see her, but she must have—"

"Never mind," April said. She looked at Clint.

"Are you feeling all right, Gladys?" Clint asked.

"Yes, I'm fine."

"A little sore from last night?"

"Huh?"

"From the dancing, I mean."

"Oh, yes, I am a little sore." She rubbed her upper arms nervously.

"Did you see Mr. Dorsett after you came upstairs, Gladys?"

"Uh . . . no, no, I didn't. I, uh, went to my room and went to sleep."

"It must have been early."

"A little early."

"And you're still tired now? After all that sleep?"

"I'm . . . I just . . . yes, I'm still tired."

"Then maybe we better let you get back to bed," Clint said.

"I—I'd appreciate it."

"Sure, Gladys."

Clint turned to go to the door, with April behind him, then stopped.

"Oh, Gladys . . ."

"Yes?" She looked up from the bed, her eyes wide.

"What did you and Mr. Dorsett talk about last night?"

"I, uh, don't remember, really."

"Nothing at all?"

"Well," Gladys said, "we, uh, flirted a little . . ." She looked at April when she said that. "I didn't mean nothing by it, Miss Donovan. . . . "

"It's okay, Gladys," April said, "really."

"Well," Clint said, "we'd better go."

"Get some more rest, Gladys," April said.

She and Clint went out the door and stood in the hall.

"That girl was lying," Clint said.

"Even I could see that," April said. "How do we get her to tell the truth?"

"I don't know," Clint said. "Did you see the way she stood, the way she sat? She's all closed up, defensive. She's afraid."

"She didn't move right, either," April said. "Clint, I'd be willing to bet that she's not sore just from dancing."

"I feel the same way."

"What do we do now? We haven't found out anything."

"Let's go someplace where we can talk," Clint suggested.

They walked to the stairs and started down, then stopped. At the bottom of the steps stood four men. Clint recognized Pullman but did not know the other men.

"They all work for Leo," April said in a whisper.

"Come on," Clint said, and they went down the rest of the steps.

"Mr. Dorsett would like to talk to you," Pullman said to Clint.

"Both of us?" April asked.

"No," Pullman said, looking directly at Clint. He pointed and said, "Just you."

"I'll wait—" April said.

"We'll take care of her," Pullman said.

"No," Clint said, "I think Miss Donovan will stay with me."

He and Pullman matched stares for a while, and then Pullman said, "Have it your way. He's in his office."

"I know the way," April said.

Pullman smiled at her and said, "Why don't we all just go, huh?"

TWENTY-SIX

April led the way to Leo Dorsett's office. She entered first, followed by Clint Adams, and then Pullman. The other men remained outside.

Dorsett stared at April for a few moments before speaking, shaking his head.

"I'm disappointed in you, April."

"I've been disappointed in you for a long time, Leo," she replied.

Pullman backed up and stood just to April's right. Clint, in turn, backed away and stood up from her left. At the moment the conversation was just between April and Leo Dorsett.

"I took you in, gave you a job, made you manager, and this is the way you repay me."

"What about the abuse, Leo?" April said. "Do I owe you for that?"

Dorsett smiled sadly and shook his head.

"There was no abuse, April."

"Tell that to my bruises, Leo. Tell it to the other girls who have bruises."

"Dancing onstage is tough work, April. Some of the girls get bruises."

"This is not for my benefit, Leo," April said. "You want Clint and Pullman to hear this. I've been on the receiving end of your hands, remember?"

"You're trying to get these men on your side, April," Dorsett said. "Tell me what I did to deserve this kind of treatment. Especially today, after the tragedy that happened to me yesterday."

"To you? I think the tragedy happened to Elsa, don't you, Leo?"

"Elsa's dead, April," Dorsett said, "and we have to survive this and keep our business going. Where were you last night, by the way?"

"None of your business."

Dorsett's face flushed.

"You belong to me in more ways than one," Dorsett said. "Don't forget that, April."

"You don't own me at all, Leo. Nobody owns anybody."

"Have you been listening to somebody, April? Don't forget I paid to bring you here. You owe me money."

"That doesn't mean you own me."

"We have a relationship."

"Is that what you call it? You force me to have sex with you and you call that a relationship?"

"I never forced you—"

"Stop it, Leo!" she said. "Clint doesn't believe you, and I'm sure Pullman knows the truth and doesn't care."

Dorsett stood up angrily.

"That's enough, April! It's time for you to remember who I am."

"I know who you are, Leo," April said.

"Then it's time for you to come back," Dorsett said. "You've only been gone one night, and I can forgive you and take you back."

"Forgive me?" she said. "I was with Clint Adams all night, Leo, in his room. I had sex with him, and he didn't force me. I had sex with him willingly, and it was wonderful—better than it's ever been with you."

Dorsett's face, already flushed, turned beet-red. He switched his gaze from April to Clint, who now stepped forward, figuring he was to be included in the conversation now.

"I was ready to be friends with you, Adams."

"I don't make friends with men who mistreat women, Dorsett."

"You don't have any proof of that."

"I'll take April's word for it."

"You're a foolish man."

"I was thinking the same thing about you."

Dorsett looked at Pullman and for a moment Clint thought he was going to give the man the word.

"Don't make the mistake of thinking you're in a controlling position here, Leo," Clint said.

There was a tense moment as everyone waited to see what was going to happen.

"April, what do you want?" Dorsett asked.

"First, I want to know who killed Elsa."

Dorsett spread his hands helplessly.

"I don't know who killed her, April," Dorsett

said. "I don't know what you said to her, but after you disappeared last night she came out on the floor to mingle. I guess she went upstairs with the wrong man."

"I couldn't get through to her, Leo. I don't believe she finally came out."

"Well, ask the other girls—"

"I have."

"And?"

"They all think she came out, but nobody actually saw her."

"That's strange," Dorsett said thoughtfully. "I could have sworn I saw Gladys talking to Elsa."

"We talked to Gladys."

"She probably just didn't remember," Dorsett said. "She wasn't feeling too well last night, and you probably woke her up. I tell you what, ask her again later and you'll probably get a different answer."

"Sure, you'll make certain of that."

"April, I don't understand where all this anger is coming from—" Dorsett started, but April cut him off.

"Do you know what scares me, Leo?" she said. "I think you really believe that."

Again, Dorsett simply spread his hands and arms, looking for all the world like a man who was totally confused. If he was acting, Clint thought, he was very good at it.

"I'll tell you what else I want," April said to Dorsett. "I want to get away from you. I want to leave town and get on with my life."

"Then do it."

"I want to do it without having to look over my

shoulder for you all the time."

"You think I'll come after you, April?"

"I know you will."

"Are you going to be leaving with him?" Dorsett asked, looking at Clint.

"Yes."

"Then I'd be foolish to come after you if you're with the Gunsmith, wouldn't I?"

"I wouldn't put anything past you, Leo."

"I think you're being foolish now, April. If you want to leave, go ahead and leave."

"I intend to, Leo," she said, "but not before I find out what happened to Elsa."

"That's the sheriff's job, April."

"Well, we're going to give him some help."

"You're in on this, Adams?"

"That's right."

"You didn't even know the girl."

"She still shouldn't be dead," Clint said.

Dorsett shook his head.

"You don't want to cross me in my own town."

"I'll do what I feel I have to do," Clint said.

"Then get out, both of you," Dorsett said. "I'm in mourning."

"Oh my God, Leo . . ." April said, shaking her head. "You're such a hypocrite."

"Open the door for them, Pullman. Miss Donovan is leaving, and I don't want her coming back here."

Pullman did as he was told. April started for the door, followed by Clint. At the door he stopped so that he and Pullman could exchange glances.

"Scared?" he asked.

"No."

"Neither am I," Clint said. "This is a waste of time."

With that he looked away and went out the door.

Dorsett sat back down behind his desk.

"What happened to that girl last night?" Pullman asked.

"Somebody killed her. That's all I know."

"Did you kill her?"

Dorsett's head snapped up and he glared at the man.

"Why are you asking me that?"

"I won't work for a man who kills women."

"When did you get a conscience?"

"I'm just asking—"

"I didn't kill her," Dorsett said. "Why would I? I'd be costing myself money."

"What do you want me to do about them?"

"Just keep an eye on them. I don't know yet if they're any kind of danger to me."

"You going to let the girl go?"

Dorsett looked away.

"Nobody leaves me, Pullman," he said tightly. "Nobody!"

TWENTY-SEVEN

Clint told April he wanted to go somewhere and talk, but not back to the hotel.

"Do you know of a café we can go to?"

"I know just the place."

She took him down a small street that had barely any foot traffic, to a small café at the very end of the street. When they looked in the window they saw only empty tables.

"How did you ever find this place?"

"I was just out walking one day and I happened to find it."

"Is the food good?"

"No."

"How about the coffee?"

She made a face.

"It's strong."

"Good. Let's go inside."

He let her go in first and looked around before

entering to see if they had been followed. If Dorsett was going to have someone keep an eye on them, he hadn't had time to do it yet.

Inside Clint directed April to a corner table. When the waiter came over, they ordered coffee.

"Just coffee?" he asked.

"Yes."

The waiter, an elderly man with a gentle smile, directed that smile at April and said, "We have some peach pie."

"All right. I'll have a piece of peach pie."

"And you, sir?"

Clint smiled.

"All right. I'll have a piece, too."

"Very good," the man said. He leaned over and added, "Confidentially, the food here is not very good, but the pie is."

"Thanks for the advice," Clint said.

The waiter walked away, and Clint and April smiled at each other.

"Peach pie," she said.

"Yeah."

"Like peach pie will solve anything."

"Maybe it won't," Clint said, "but maybe it will be good."

The waiter returned with a tray bearing coffee and two slices of peach pie.

"Please enjoy it," the man said, and faded away.

They each tasted the pie and found it surprisingly good. Clint also enjoyed the coffee.

"Clint, what are we going to do?"

"I think we have to talk to Gladys again."

"I doubt we'll get the chance," she said. "Leo won't let us get anywhere near her."

"We'll have to try and get around him."

"Him and Pullman," April reminded him.

"Yes, Pullman. I don't know anything about him, April. Do you?"

"He's a very capable man, Clint," April said. "I've seen him beat up three or four men at a time with his fists, and I think he's at least as good with a gun."

"And he has help."

"Lots of it," she said, "and Leo has the money to hire even more."

"I think he would only do that if he felt physically threatened," Clint said. "We just won't give him cause to."

"You're giving him too much credit," April said. "He could have somebody shoot you from hiding."

A small shiver ran up and down Clint's back, but he kept it from showing. The worst—and possibly only—fear of his life was being shot in the back, the way his friend Wild Bill Hickok had been.

"Aren't you the one who told me that his violence was directed toward women?"

"Yes, his *personal* violence. He's had Pullman beat up more men than I can count—and I think he'd have him do a lot more than beat you up."

"Well, let's just take care of that problem when it comes up," Clint said. "Right now we've got to figure out a way to get to Gladys without encountering either Dorsett or Pullman."

TWENTY-EIGHT

As Clint and April walked back to the main street from the café, Clint saw Sheriff Osborne walking down the street.

"I've been looking all over town for you," Osborne said as he reached them. "Have you been hidin' out?"

"We had some peach pie, Sheriff Osborne," Clint said. "What can I do for you?"

"Somebody wants to talk to you."

"Oh? Who?"

Osborne looked at April.

"Could you, uh, excuse us, Miss Donovan?"

"Where am I supposed to go?"

"Just stand here a minute," Osborne said. He took Clint's elbow and walked him away a few feet.

"What's this about?"

"A man wants to see you."

"What man?"

"His name is Kline, Mr. Parker Kline."

"Am I supposed to know him?"

"No, I guess not. He owns The Crystal Palace."

"So?"

"He and Leo Dorsett are competitors."

"And he wants to talk to me about what?"

"I think he'll have to tell you that."

"Where is this conversation supposed to take place?"

"In his office," Osborne said, then added, "if you'll go."

"Why not? I meant to take a look at the other places in town."

"There's only two places worth looking at," Osborne said. "Dorsett's and The Crystal Palace."

"Well, I've seen plenty of one," Clint said. "I might as well go and see the other one."

"I'll walk over there with you."

"Why? I think I can find my way. And if I can't, April will take me."

"You're not taking her with you."

"Yes, I am."

"Why?"

"Because it's not safe for me to leave her."

"Why not?"

"You figure it out, Sheriff," Clint said. "Meanwhile, I'll find my own way over to The Crystal Palace, if you don't mind."

"Sure, sure, go ahead," Osborne said. "I was just delivering a message."

As Osborne walked away, Clint felt bad that a man with that many years behind a badge was reduced to delivering messages.

Clint walked over to where April was standing. "Do you know Parker Kline?"

"Sure, I do," she said. "His place is Leo's biggest competition."

"He wants to talk to me."

"About what?"

"I don't know. I guess the only way to find out is to go and see him."

"Do you want me to come with you?"

"Do you have a problem with that?"

"No," she said, "Parker's always been very respectful to me. In fact, more than once he's tried to hire me away from Leo."

"Maybe he'll make another offer."

"You're the one he wants to see. Maybe he wants to hire you."

"I'm not for hire."

"I know," she said, smiling, "you only work for—"

"Don't say it," he said. "Come on, show me where this Crystal Palace is."

TWENTY-NINE

April walked Clint down the street for about four blocks, a respectful distance from Leo Dorsett's Dream Palace. As they entered he noticed that Kline's saloon was set up very much the same way as The Dream Palace.

"Which place opened first?" Clint asked her.

"You noticed the similarities, huh? They opened a month apart."

"But which one opened first?"

"Well, the way I heard it, Leo opened first, but Parker actually started construction first."

"Then how did Leo finish first?"

She hesitated, then said, "There was something about a fire . . ."

"Oh."

There were very few customers at this time of the afternoon, but Clint and April drew their attention as they entered—or rather April did.

They walked to the bar where the bartender was giving them a funny look.

"Miss Donovan," he said, "it's not often we get a visit from our competitors."

"Hello, Hal."

Hal was tall, thin, sandy-haired, in his early thirties.

"This isn't exactly a visit," April added.

"I have to see Mr. Kline," Clint said.

"And you are . . . ?" Hal asked, looking Clint up and down.

"Clint Adams. I heard from Sheriff Osborne that Mr. Kline wanted to talk to me about something."

"Adams . . . oh," Hal said, backing up a step. "Uh, I'll tell the boss you're, uh, here. Wait . . . uh, wait here."

As Hal moved out from behind the bar, April said, "He recognized your name."

"You think so?"

"Well, of course. He was scared." She turned to look at him. "Are you used to that reaction?"

Clint shrugged, preferring not to talk about it, but she wouldn't let it go.

"How can you live knowing people are afraid every time they hear your name?"

"I just try to do what I can to show them that there is nothing to be afraid of."

"That's kind of hard, isn't it? When you have a reputation for killing people?"

"Are you afraid of me, April?"

"No, of course not."

"Then I guess it's not so hard, is it?"

She frowned and Hal returned before she could reply.

"The boss says for you to go on up," he said. "Up the stairs, first door at the top."

"Thanks."

"Miss Donovan, he asked if Mr. Adams would go up alone," Hal said apologetically.

"No," Clint said, "she'll be coming up with me."

Hal turned and looked at Clint for a moment before answering.

"Well . . . uh, suit yourself, Mr. Adams. You can, uh, explain it to the boss yourself."

"Don't worry, Hal," Clint said, "I'll see to it that he knows it was my idea."

"Uh, thank you kindly, Mr. Adams."

"Let's go," April said, shaking her head in disgust at the fear Hal was showing.

She led the way to the stairs and Clint climbed them behind her. At the top she knocked and waited for the muffled, "Come in," from inside before opening the door.

"Miss Donovan," a man's voice said from inside.

Clint stepped into the room after April and saw the man who had spoken. He was tall and well dressed in a blue three-piece suit. Hanging from the vest pocket was a gold chain Clint assumed was connected to a gold watch. Kline was in his fifties, well fed but not fat. His hair was bushy and gray, and he had a neatly groomed mustache that completely obscured his upper lip from view.

"Mr. Adams?"

"That's right."

The man came around the desk and extended his hand. His handshake was very firm.

"My name is Parker Kline. I, uh, had asked that you come up alone."

"I can't afford to leave Miss Donovan alone, Mr. Kline."

"Oh? Is there a problem?"

"I've left Leo, Parker," April said.

Kline looked surprised.

"He can't be too happy about that."

"He's not," Clint said.

"I wouldn't think so," Kline said. He looked at Clint and asked, "Have you met Pullman?"

"I have."

Kline nodded and thought for a moment.

"Well then, sit down, both of you," he said finally. "We have more to talk about than I originally thought."

THIRTY

"What do we have to talk about, Mr. Kline?" Clint asked.

"First, let me offer you something. Coffee? A drink?" Kline said.

"Nothing for me, thanks."

"No, thank you," April said.

"Why don't we just get to it," Clint suggested.

"Very well," Kline said. He sat back in his big leather chair and folded his hands across his belly. "I hadn't heard about your trouble with Leo, Miss Donovan," he said, then directed his attention at Clint, "but I had heard that you were in town."

"What made you think I was having trouble with Dorsett?" Clint asked.

"Pullman," Kline said. "Dorsett only calls for Pullman when he's got trouble."

"What's it to you, then?"

"I figure two ways," Kline said. "One, you might end up working for Dorsett. Before that happens I want to offer you a job with me. You see, I know your reputation."

"Everyone seems to," April said.

Clint ignored the remark.

"What's the second way?" Clint asked.

"You're going to end up going against Dorsett, which means going up against Pullman and his men."

"So?"

"I could offer you help."

"Why?"

"Let's just say it would be in my best interests to, uh, inconvenience Leo Dorsett. But let's deal with first things first. Would you consider working for me?"

"I don't hire out my gun."

"Why do you think I want to hire you for your gun?" Kline asked.

"You're offering me a job based on my reputation, Mr. Kline," Clint said. "What other reason could you have for wanting to hire me?"

Kline studied Clint for a moment then said, "I fear I've insulted you."

"Misjudged is more like it."

"I apologize."

Clint waved the apology—and the offense— away.

"To the second point, then," Kline said. "Would you accept my help?"

"If I need it."

"You don't think you will?"

"I don't know yet that things will come to violence," Clint said. "That is what you're offering me, isn't it? To back me up in that case?"

"Of course. I can offer you several men who are quite good with a gun."

"Do you have a Pullman, too?"

Kline smiled.

"I have men who work for me, Mr. Adams. None of them, I'm afraid, is like Mr. Pullman. I fear when the time comes he will be your responsibility."

"That suits me," Clint said. "He'd be the one I concentrated on anyway."

"Then you'll let me help."

"I'll let you know."

Kline raised a hand and said, "My men will be at your disposal at a moment's notice."

"Fine."

"And now to you, my dear," Kline said.

"Me?"

"Yes. It's no secret that I have wanted you to work for me for some time," the man said. "Now would seem to be a most opportune time to make the offer again."

April didn't say anything.

"Well, I'm already ahead of the game," Kline said. "In the past you've turned me down without consideration."

"I have to think about it."

"Excellent," Kline said, clapping his hands together. "You do that. Think it over and let me know. I assume your other option is leaving town? Or has Molly Haywood already made an offer for your services?"

"I haven't talked to Molly."

"Well, rest assured, you'll hear from her."

"What would I be doing for you, Mr. Kline?"

"The same kinds of things you were doing for Leo, my dear. Handling the girls . . . oh, and of course there would be no, uh, obligation on your part . . . if you know what I mean?"

"I do."

"Good," Kline said. He looked at both of them in turn and added, "We all understand each other."

"Yes, we do," Clint said.

They all stood up, but Kline remained behind his desk while Clint and April walked to the door.

"Thank you for coming to see me," Kline said as Clint opened the door, "both of you."

"We'll be in touch," Clint said, and he and April went out.

As they passed the bar, Hal called out, "Drink on the house?"

Clint looked at April, then said to Hal, "A beer would be nice."

"Make it two," April said.

Hal brought them their beer then faded to the other side of the bar.

"I think it would be a good idea for you to accept Kline's offer of a job," Clint said.

"Why?"

"He could protect you," Clint said. "You wouldn't have to leave here, and Dorsett couldn't get to you."

"How long could I live like that?"

"At least until we settle with Dorsett," Clint said. "April, I'll be able to move around better without you, and when the time comes—if the time comes—for violence, I won't have to worry about you."

"I can take care of myself."

Clint stared at her.

"Okay, so I can't take care of myself, but—"

"Just think it over," Clint said. "You don't have to decide anything today."

April sulked over her beer, which she sipped daintily.

"Who's Molly?"

"Molly Haywood," she said. "She owns the Gold River, at the other end of town."

"Another place like this and Dorsett's?"

"Yes."

"Run by a woman?"

"Owned and run by a woman," April said. "What's wrong with that? If I had the money I'd open my own place, too."

"I didn't mean any offense," Clint said. "Take it easy."

"I'm sorry, I didn't mean to snap at you. It's just that I've proven that I can run a business, and all I ever got for it was . . ."

"Abuse?"

She nodded.

"What kind of man is Kline?"

"Fair," she said.

"Why didn't you ever accept his offer of a job before?"

"The same reason I never left Leo before."

"But now you have left Leo. I'll bet you could get Kline to pay you more than Leo was."

"Without a doubt."

"And what about Molly Haywood?"

"Same thing."

"Sounds to me like everybody thinks you're the reason for The Dream Palace's success."

"I guess I was."

Clint finished his beer. April's was still half full.

"You going to finish that?"

"No," she said, pushing it away. "I don't really like beer much."

"Then let's go."

"Where?"

"I'm not sure yet. Maybe we should go and talk to Molly Haywood."

"About what?"

"About a job, and about backing my play."

"Then you do think this will become violent?"

"If Pullman wasn't involved, I probably wouldn't. He makes the difference."

"You don't even know him, how can you make a judgment like that?"

"I know his type, April," Clint said. "I've dealt with them many times before."

"And killed them?"

"Some of them."

"Are you going to kill Pullman?"

"Not if I don't have to."

"But if you have to, you will?"

"I always do what I have to do."

"This is all because I wanted to leave Leo," she said. "I don't want people getting killed just so I can be free of him."

"What about Elsa?" Clint asked. "Her death had nothing to do with that. Don't you still want to find out what happened to her?"

"Of course."

"All right, then," Clint said. "Let's go and talk to Molly Haywood. In the meantime we can try to think of some way to get Gladys away from Leo long enough to get the truth out of her."

"All right."

"And maybe you can think of one of the other girls, maybe one who's been with you the longest, who might help us as well."

"How?"

"I don't know, but who would the girls be loyal to, you or Leo?"

"They'd probably be loyal to me," she said, "but they're afraid of Leo."

Clint was afraid that when it came to a contest between loyalty and fear, fear would win.

THIRTY-ONE

Molly Haywood's Gold River is what it said above the door. Clint doubted she had much gold, though, because her place—at least from the outside—could hardly match either Leo Dorsett's or Parker Kline's in grandeur.

"It looks like a regular saloon," Clint said.

"It is, but it doesn't have regular saloon entertainment," April said.

"Same as both palaces?" Clint asked. It hadn't escaped his notice that Dorsett and Kline had both called their places "palaces"—he put that down to no imagination.

"The same, but it's too early for it now."

"Let's just go inside and see if the proprietor will talk to us."

"Oh, she will," April said. "Molly and I are friends."

"Then maybe this would be a good place for you

123

to lay low until this is all over," Clint said. "Why didn't you tell me that before?"

"You didn't ask me."

They went inside and Clint saw that the setup was that of a conventional saloon, with a few gaming tables interspersed. The bar was pitted and old, not at all like the expensive bars in the other two places.

"Hello, Miss Donovan," the bartender said.

Clint was starting to think that every bartender in town knew her.

"Hello, Dugan," she said.

"And what would a fine-lookin' lass like you be doin' here at this hour?" the man asked. His Irish accent went with his red hair and freckles.

"I'm looking for Molly. Is she around?"

"Upstairs, in her office. You know where it is. She'll be glad to see you. She's been wonderin' about you—wonderin' and worryin'."

"Thanks, Dugan."

"Who's yer friend?"

"Clint Adams." Clint extended his hand.

"Dugan," the bartender said, shaking it. "Pleasure to make your acquaintance, Mr. Adams."

If the man recognized Clint's name, he was hiding it well.

Once again Clint followed April. It seemed to him he had been doing that for days, not just hours. They went upstairs and April knocked on the door of Molly Haywood's office. Instead of calling out, Molly answered the door herself.

Clint was surprised. For some reason he had expected an older woman. Molly Haywood was older than April, but not by much. Clint guessed she was still on the safe side of forty, although she looked younger. She was tall, dark-haired, with smooth, pale skin, red lips, and a full bosom.

"April!" she exclaimed and grabbed the younger woman in a hug. "Where have you been?" she asked, holding April at arm's length.

"Hi, Molly. Can we talk to you for a minute?"

"Sure. Who's your good-looking friend?"

"His name is Clint Adams."

They entered the office and Molly closed the door. She turned then and shook hands with Clint like a man. It was the only thing she did like a man. He noticed that her eyes were brown and set just a bit too widely apart. Also, her nose was a bit too big. However, taken as a whole instead of part by part, she had a face that could best be described as . . . arresting.

"I heard about the commotion over at Leo's," Molly said. She was talking to April, but still looking into Clint's eyes.

"Poor Elsa," April said.

"A new girl?" Now she looked at the other woman.

"Yes," April said. "Her first night."

"Who did it?"

"I don't know," April said. "I wasn't there."

"Where were you?"

April looked at Clint, and Molly smiled.

"I see," Molly said. "All night, huh?"

"And this morning," April said. "I mean, we've been together all morning—I mean, trying to find out—"

"Relax, honey," Molly said, "you don't have to explain anything to me. Sit down, both of you, and tell me what's on your mind."

There was a sofa in the room and another soft armchair. Both women sat on the sofa, while Clint took the chair. The interior of the office was furnished much more tastefully and expensively than the rest of the saloon.

Clint left it to April to tell Molly what they were doing, and once or twice Molly glanced over at Clint and gave him an appraising sort of look.

"So, Clint here is trying to help you get away from Leo?"

"That's right."

"Honey, why didn't you ever tell me what that bastard was doing to you?"

April looked away.

"I was ashamed."

"What did you have to be ashamed of?"

"I was ashamed that I was letting him do it to me, Molly."

"Honey . . ." Molly said, leaning forward to put her hand on her friend's. She looked at Clint and said, "Thanks for what you're doing for her, Mr. Adams. Makes you kind of a special man."

"Call me Clint. I don't know how special I am, Molly, but there's something you can do to help us."

"Like what?"

"Keep April here."

"Clint—"

He ignored April's protests.

"You think she's in danger?"

"I don't know," Clint said, "but I know that Dorsett's called in his man, Pullman."

"That means there's gonna be trouble for sure," Molly said.

"If there is, I don't want April around if lead starts flying," Clint said. "Can you protect her here?"

"I sure can," Molly said. "I've got some men of my own I can count on. Fact is, I could probably loan you a few, if you need them."

"I might take you up on that, Molly."

He stood up.

"Where are you going?" April asked.

"I think Dorsett and I should have a talk, just the two of us."

"I want to go with you," she said, standing up.

"I want you to stay here, April," Clint said. "Molly will take good care of you."

"I want to go with you," she said, like a petulant child.

"April, let the man do what he has to do to get you free of that bastard."

"Maybe I can find out what happened to Elsa if I'm there alone," Clint said.

"You think he killed that girl?" Molly asked.

"Him, or some nameless, faceless cowboy who's left town," Clint said.

"Elsa wouldn't have gone upstairs with anyone," April said. "I'm sure of that."

"Then he did it, the scum," Molly said.

"If he did," Clint said, "I'll prove it, and the law will put him away."

"Can't say as that would make me break into tears," Molly said. "Have you talked with Parker Kline yet?"

"We have," Clint said, "and he made me the same offer of help."

"You'll have a lot of men backing your play, then, if it comes to that."

"Before that happens," Clint said, "I'd like to try and wrap this up just between me and Dorsett."

"Clint," April said, grabbing his arm, "be careful. Leo keeps a gun in his desk."

"Has he ever used it?"

"Not that I know of."

"Thanks for the warning."

"Sit back down, April," Molly said. "Let the man go and do what he's got to do."

"Thanks, Molly."

"You just be sure to come back, you hear?" Molly said.

"I'll be back," Clint promised both of them.

THIRTY-TWO

When Pullman entered his office, Leo Dorsett looked up from his desk.

"What?"

"We didn't pick them up when they left, but soon after."

"And?"

"They went to see Parker Kline."

"I knew it!" Dorsett snapped. "I knew Kline would find some way to get into it. Whose idea was it?"

"I'm not sure, but they went to see Kline right after the sheriff talked to them in the street."

"That goddamn lawman, he'll do anything for money. I'll bet he was Kline's messenger."

"That's what I figured."

"Where'd they go after that?"

"The other end of town."

Dorsett frowned, then asked, "Molly Haywood?"

"Right."

"That bitch!" Dorsett slammed his fist down on the desk. "She and Kline are both after my blood."

Pullman didn't respond. He knew that, given the chance, Dorsett would have gone after them as well.

"Adams is going to be hard to take care of if he's got people from Kline and Haywood backing his play," Pullman said.

"I know that."

"I think I should take care of him now."

Dorsett rubbed his hand over his face.

"If only April hadn't gone to him for help," he said. "He'd just ride out and that would be the end of it."

"He could still do that," Pullman said.

"What do you mean?"

"Let him ride out."

"With April?"

"You've got plenty of other women."

"Not like April."

Pullman made a face.

"One woman is the same as another when they're lying in bed."

"April is more than that, Pullman," Dorsett said. "She helps keep this place running, she keeps the girls in line . . . she does the books . . ."

Pullman scowled. He didn't have any respect for a man who let a woman run that much of his life. According to what April Donovan had said earlier, Dorsett also wasn't above abusing the girls, and maybe beating some of them. Pullman was thinking that maybe, after this was over, it would be time to pull up stakes and move on. Working for Leo Dorsett was no longer such an attractive prospect. Maybe New York, or someplace like that, where men were more civilized.

"You want me to kill Adams or not?" he asked.

"I don't know," Dorsett said. "Get out and let me think."

"Don't take too long," Pullman said, opening the office door.

"There's time, Pullman," Dorsett said, sitting slumped in his chair, "there's plenty of time."

"Maybe not," Pullman said, looking out into the saloon.

"What do you mean?"

"Adams just walked in."

Dorsett scowled.

"Is April with him?"

"No."

"He must have left her somewhere," Dorsett said. "Close the door before he sees you."

Pullman obeyed.

"Go out the back and find April."

"What do you want me to do with her?"

Dorsett gave Pullman a withering stare and said, "Find out where she is."

"Right."

Pullman went to the rear door and went out. Dorsett remained behind his desk, wondering if he should go out and see Adams or wait there for him. He decided to wait.

He opened the top drawer of his desk, touched the .32 caliber Colt that lay within, then closed the drawer partway and settled down to wait.

THIRTY-THREE

Clint entered The Dream Palace and was struck at the same time by the similarities to The Crystal Palace and the differences in comparison to the Gold River.

"Back so soon?" Jake asked.

"Yes."

"Where's Miss Donovan?"

"She's . . . resting."

"Beer?"

Clint's intention had been to speak with Dorsett immediately, but now he decided to talk to the bartender for a while.

"Sure, a beer would be fine," Clint said.

He looked around and saw that the place was starting to come to life. It would be a few hours yet before people started to arrive in earnest, before the gambling would start, and a few more hours after that before the "entertainment" would commence.

"Thanks . . . Jake, isn't it?"

"That's right."

"Jake, do you know all the women—the entertainers?" Clint asked.

"Most of them."

"What about the girl who was killed?"

"Elsa," Jake said. "Didn't know her real well. She and two others were only hired yesterday. Last night was the first time they danced."

"Did you see Elsa last night, after she danced?"

Jake frowned.

"I can't say."

"Why not? Either you saw her or you didn't."

"Well, if she went upstairs with a man—who then killed her—then she must have come out . . ."

"But . . ."

"But I don't remember seeing her."

"Which means you didn't."

"Uh . . . probably not, no."

"Do you remember seeing the other girls?"

The bartender thought a moment then said, "Um, well, yeah, I guess so . . ."

"Gladys?"

"The big blonde? Oh yeah, I saw her."

"Did she go upstairs with a man?"

"Um, that depends on what you mean by . . . a man."

Clint frowned.

"What do you mean by that?"

"Well, I saw Gladys sitting with the boss."

"At which table?"

"Well, his table."

"That one over there?" Clint pointed to the table at which he had sat with April and Dorsett the night before.

"That's right."

"Was Miss Donovan with them?"

"No. She got up and left the table before Gladys walked over to sit."

"Where did April go?"

"Through that door," Jake said, pointing to the back.

There were two doors back there, one of which led to Dorsett's office. Jake the bartender was pointing to the other one.

"Where does that lead?" Clint asked.

"Back behind the stage. There are some rooms back there where the girls dress."

"Did she come back out?"

"Not that I saw."

"And how long did Gladys sit with the boss?"

"Not long."

"And then what?"

"And then she went . . . upstairs."

"Upstairs . . . alone?"

"Yes."

"Is she supposed to do that?"

"What?"

"Go upstairs alone. Aren't the girls supposed to take a paying customer with them?"

"You've got the wrong idea, Mr. Adams."

"Do I?"

"The girls don't have to go upstairs unless they want to."

"But they do get paid."

"Well . . . yes."

"And they give the money to Mr. Dorsett."

"Well, sure. After all, he's the boss."

"Right," Clint said. "So Gladys went up alone?"

"That's right."

"And what did Mr. Dorsett do?"

"Um . . . I don't know why I should be talking about this," Jake said.

"All of a sudden?"

"Well . . ."

"Isn't that what bartenders are supposed to do?" Clint asked. "Talk?"

"Well . . ." Jake said, with a sheepish grin, "I guess we do . . ."

"So what did the boss do after Gladys went upstairs?" Clint asked.

"Well, he got up and went backstage."

"And then what?"

"I don't know," Jake said. "I didn't see him the rest of the night."

"And the others? Did you see Elsa or Gladys the rest of the night?"

Jake thought a moment, then said, "I don't think I did."

"Do you think that Gladys went up to her own room?" Clint asked.

"Well . . ."

"Or to Mr. Dorsett's room?"

Jake just smiled and shrugged.

"Mr. Dorsett has been known to take a woman or two to his room, hasn't he?"

"It's no secret the boss likes women," Jake said.

"Like Miss Donovan?"

"Usually," Jake said, and then added, "but not always."

Clint finished his beer, which he'd been sipping all along.

"Is he around? The boss?"

"I think he's in his office. Want me to check?"

"Please."

Jake brought his massive bulk out from behind the bar and waddled over to the office door. He knocked, stuck his head in, and exchanged a few words, then closed the door and came back to the bar.

"He's in there. He says you should go ahead in."

"Thanks, Jake . . . for the conversation and for the beer."

"Sure."

Clint left the bar, walked to the office door, and knocked.

THIRTY-FOUR

Dorsett called out for Clint to enter, and he did.

"You're back," Dorsett said.

"Obviously."

"To kill me?"

Clint laughed.

"Why would I want to do that?"

"You're April's new lover," Dorsett said, "and I'm the old one."

"That's no reason to kill a man."

"Isn't it?"

Clint looked around and saw Dorsett's small bar against the wall.

"Do you mind?"

Dorsett looked, then said, "Not if you pour me one, too."

"Brandy?" Clint asked, walking over.

"The best brandy."

Clint poured two glasses and brought one over

to Dorsett, then sat down opposite the man.

"Where's your man?"

"Who's that?"

"Pullman."

"You worried about Pullman?"

"Of course I am," Clint said. "I understand he's a very capable man."

"Oh, he is. That's why I employ him."

"So where is he?"

"Oh, he's around."

"Do you have him out looking for April?"

"Why would I have him doing that?" Dorsett said. "The woman walked out. The hell with her."

"I don't think that's what you really feel, Dorsett," Clint said.

"What do you know about me, Adams?"

"Well, I know you brutalize women."

"That's a lie April's been telling you."

"I've seen your work, Dorsett."

"You won't find another woman in this building who would tell you that I hit her. It's April's word against mine."

"Maybe . . ."

"What do you want, Adams?"

"I want your assurance that you won't go after April Donovan."

"Why would I go after her, especially if she's leaving with you?"

"What if she doesn't leave with me? In fact, what if she doesn't leave town at all?"

"What? I thought she was going with you."

"Look, in spite of what you think, Dorsett, April is not leaving you for me—she's just leaving. She doesn't want to put up with your abuse anymore."

"Here we go again, talking about abuse. Why do you believe her and not me?"

"Well," Clint said, "I've got to believe one of you, and I choose her."

"You're making the wrong choice."

"Maybe," Clint said, "but it's my choice to make, isn't it?"

"I don't understand why you came here, Adams."

"I want to talk about Elsa."

That surprised Dorsett.

"Why do you want to talk about her?"

"I'd like to know who killed her."

"So would I. He cost me my investment. Yesterday was her first day, you know. I didn't hardly get my money's worth out of her."

"Too bad," Clint said. "I'm sure she's all upset."

"What are you talking about? She's dead."

"Wherever she is," Clint said, "I'm sure she's upset that she let you down."

Dorsett obviously did not believe in any kind of hereafter, because Clint's words were confounding him.

"You know, Leo," Clint said, "nobody saw her come out onto the floor last night."

"So? Nobody remembers seeing her. That doesn't mean she wasn't there."

"Maybe not."

"I didn't see her."

Clint frowned and said, "I . . . don't think I believe you, Leo."

"Look—who said you could call me by my first name?" Dorsett suddenly complained.

"Come on, Leo," Clint said, "it's just you and

me here. What's the difference?"

Dorsett looked down at the desk drawer the .32 was in. He wondered if he could get it out in time against Adams. He doubted it. He should have kept it in his lap.

"Let's get back to Elsa."

"What about her?"

"You sent April back to talk to her."

"So?"

"While she was gone, Gladys came over to sit with you."

"Lots of the girls sit with me."

"This one you sent up to your room to wait for you," Clint said.

"Who told you that?"

"Is it true?"

Dorsett thought about it for a moment, then said, "What if it is? Who told you?"

"Lucky guess, Leo. She's quite a woman, that Gladys."

Dorsett didn't answer.

"Was she quite a woman last night?"

No answer.

"Or did you not get to your room?"

"What are you talking about?"

"I'll tell you what, Leo," Clint said, leaning forward. "I think you killed Elsa."

"What?"

"That's what I think."

"There's no way you can prove that," Dorsett said, eyeing the top drawer again.

"There's one way."

"How's that?"

"If someone saw you," Clint said. "All I'd have to do is find them."

"No one saw me."

"Then you did kill her?"

"No one saw me because I didn't do it."

Clint stared at Dorsett and said, "I think you did."

"You're crazy."

"Maybe you didn't mean it," Clint said. "You like to hit women. Maybe you hit her too hard."

"Get out." Dorsett looked at the drawer with the gun again.

"You're not going to need that gun, Leo."

Dorsett jerked his eyes away from the drawer.

"I'd hate to see you try to get to it."

"I don't know what—no, you wouldn't hate to see me go for it." Dorsett decided not to deny the gun. April knew it was there and had probably warned Clint Adams. Knowing that, Dorsett carefully placed his empty hands on top of the desk, palms flat.

"You'd like me to go for a gun so you could kill me," Dorsett said.

"Why would I need you to do that?" Clint asked. "We're alone here. I could kill you, then take the gun out of the drawer and set it down by your body."

"You wouldn't," Dorsett said, but he didn't look confident.

"You're right," Clint said, "I wouldn't—not now, anyway. Not while there's still a chance of proving that you killed that girl."

"You can't prove it, because I didn't do it."

"Then who did?"

"Some cowboy probably. He's long gone by now."

Clint finished his brandy, put the empty glass on the desk, and stood up.

"Leo, I want you to leave April alone."

"Is she leaving town or not?"

"I don't know," Clint said. "She's had a couple of job offers."

"That bastard Kline, you mean. And that bitch Molly Haywood?"

"What's it matter who offered her the job?" Clint asked. "If she takes another job I want you to leave her alone."

"Look, Adams, I already told you and her, if she wants to leave, she can leave."

"She already has."

"Then that's that, isn't it?"

"I hope so."

Keeping his hands flat on the desk, Dorsett asked, "Are you going to stay around to make sure?"

"For a while," Clint said, "but wherever I go, I won't be too far to come back."

"Is that a threat?"

"It sure is," Clint said. "If you touch April, and I hear about it, I'll be back, and then you might have to go for that gun in your desk drawer."

Leo Dorsett looked down at the drawer, then back at Clint.

"You got a good memory, Leo?"

"Why?"

"I want to make sure you can remember everything I've just told you."

"You accused me of murder," Dorsett said. "I remember that."

"Good," Clint said, "then you can probably remember the rest of it."

THIRTY-FIVE

Clint didn't know what he'd accomplished. Would Dorsett heed his warning? Or would he now take the opportunity to send Pullman after him? And what about what he'd said to Dorsett about Elsa? Did he believe it himself?

He waved at Jake and went back outside. Instead of going back to Molly's, though, he crossed the street and walked to the sheriff's office. He found Osborne sitting behind his desk with a cup of coffee.

"You drink a lot of coffee," he said.

"I like coffee. Want some?"

"No." He sat opposite Osborne. "I just had a talk with Leo Dorsett."

"About what?"

"Elsa."

"Who?"

"The girl who was killed."

"And?"

"I think he did it."

Osborne hesitated.

"You think Leo killed one of his own girls?"

"Yes."

"Why?"

"He likes to hurt women," Clint said. "Maybe he didn't mean it, but I think he did it, all right."

"I can't arrest him just because you think he did it. I'd need a witness."

"I'll get you one."

"Who?"

"When I know, you'll know."

"Did you and Miss Donovan talk to the other girls?"

"Yes."

"And?"

"None of them will admit anything."

"Then that's it."

"You mean you're giving up?" Not that the lawman had done much up to now.

"Unless you can come up with your witness."

"Why don't you question him?"

Osborne looked disgusted.

"I wouldn't know what questions to ask."

"Osborne . . . who are you working for?"

"What do you mean?"

"I think you know."

Osborne sat forward so quickly he knocked over his coffee cup. Coffee spilled across his desk but he ignored it.

"Are you accusing me of taking money?"

"I don't have to accuse you," Clint said. "I've already been told that you do."

"By who?"

"That doesn't matter. Didn't you already deliver a message to me from Parker Kline? That's not your job, is it?"

"Don't try to tell me my job, Adams," Osborne said.

"Why not? I'm doing it for you, aren't I?"

Osborne pointed a finger at Clint.

"You asked me to let you and Miss Donovan question her girls. I did that. What have you come up with?"

"Nothing, so far."

"When you do come up with something, I'll act on it," Osborne said. "Why don't you get out of here now? I don't want to talk to you anymore."

"Sheriff—"

"If you say anything else, Mr. Adams, I may be forced to ask you to leave town. I don't think either one of us wants that kind of confrontation right now . . . do you?"

Clint studied the sheriff for a moment, then said, "No, not now."

Osborne looked down at his desk and said, "Shit, I've got to clean this up."

Clint left the sheriff trying to soak up the coffee on his desk with wanted posters.

THIRTY-SIX

Pullman waited outside the Gold River for the man he'd sent inside to do his job. He'd done the same thing at The Crystal Palace, sent a man inside to find out what he wanted to know. He knew that as soon as he entered either place he'd be recognized, and nobody would talk freely.

The man he'd sent inside both places was named Mike Connelly. As Pullman watched the front of the Gold River from across the street, Connelly came out and started across.

"Well?" Pullman asked.

"She went in, all right, but nobody's seen her come out."

At The Crystal Palace she'd been seen going in and coming out. This meant that she was still inside the Gold River.

"Okay, then," Pullman said. "Stay here and watch the place."

147

"And if she comes out?"

"Just follow her . . . but don't let her see you."

"Okay, but what if I see Adams?"

"Same thing. Don't let him see you. If he comes back here and then leaves alone, don't follow him. Don't leave here unless she does, is that understood?"

"I gotcha."

Pullman nodded and left Connelly there. He went back to The Dream Palace to tell Leo Dorsett where April Donovan was.

As he entered Dorsett's office, Pullman knew something was wrong. Dorsett was seated behind his desk and didn't even look up when he entered.

"You were right," Dorsett said without looking at him.

"What was I right about?" Pullman asked.

"Clint Adams," Dorsett said. "It's time to kill him."

"What changed your mind?"

Dorsett looked at him.

"Never mind that, just do it."

"How?"

"I don't care how."

"Do you want it to look like an accident?"

"I want him dead," Dorsett said, "and I don't care how you go about it. Is that clear enough?"

"It's gonna cost you," Pullman said.

"I don't care," Dorsett said. "It'll be worth it . . . well worth it."

THIRTY-SEVEN

Clint went back to Molly Haywood's Gold River and found April and Molly in her office, talking. Before going into the place, however, he noticed the man standing in the doorway across the street.

"Can we get to a front window?" he asked Molly as she opened the door.

"Hello to you, too. What's wrong?"

"There's someone I want you to take a look at."

"Me, too?" April asked.

Clint nodded.

"You might know him."

The three of them left the room and Molly took them to one that had a window overlooking the street.

"There's a man standing in a doorway across the street," Clint said. "He's watching the place."

Molly leaned forward to look out the window,

standing right next to Clint. He was acutely aware of her firm body next to him, her scent in his nostrils.

"Can you see him?"

"I see the son of a bitch."

"Know him?"

She moved away from the window and stood up straight.

"His name is Mike Connelly. He works with Leo Dorsett, usually with Pullman."

"He knows I'm here," April said.

Molly turned and looked at her.

"It doesn't matter. They can't get to you here . . . not unless they storm the place."

April gave Clint a look that asked if they would do that.

"I don't think there's any danger of that."

"Where did you go?" April asked. "You were gone a long time."

"Let's go back into Molly's office and I'll tell you all about it."

Clint took one last look out the window, and then followed the women out of the room.

When they got back to Molly's office, she hesitated before joining them in the room and called downstairs for three beers. Clint waited until they were all seated with frosty mugs in their hands, then he began.

First he related his conversation with Leo Dorsett, explaining why he had come right out and accused the man of killing Elsa himself.

"It makes sense to me," he said. "He has the reputation for violence against women, and she was beaten to death. After you left, April, he and Elsa were not seen again."

"April?" Molly asked. "You know Leo best. Is he capable of murder?"

"The way Clint is suggesting? Definitely."

"Did you talk to the sheriff about this?" Molly asked.

"I did. He won't do anything unless I can get a witness to the murder."

"Where are we going to find a witness?" April asked.

"Gladys."

"Who?" Molly asked.

"One of the new girls," April said.

"I think she saw what happened. That's why she appeared so scared when we talked to her."

"What makes you think she saw anything?" April asked.

He told them what the bartender had told him about Gladys sitting with Dorsett and then going directly upstairs.

"You think she went to Leo's room?" April asked.

"Yes."

"I wouldn't doubt that," April said, "except . . ."

"Except what?"

"Well, when we were auditioning the girls I would swear that Leo was interested in Elsa."

"How interested?"

"*Very* interested."

"According to Jake, as soon as Gladys went upstairs, Dorsett left his table and went into the back."

"To talk to Elsa," April said.

"Or maybe do more than talk to her," Molly suggested.

"Maybe," Clint said. "April, when Dorsett spent, uh, time with one of the girls where would it be?"

"In his room."

"So if he took Elsa up there, and Gladys was already there . . ."

"Then Gladys saw what happened," April said.

"You have to get to Gladys," Molly said.

"Right," Clint agreed. "We've got to come up with a way to get her away from Dorsett."

"You're gonna need help," Molly said. "I can let you have some of my men."

"A diversion," Clint said. "We'll need some kind of a diversion . . ."

"You look like you're getting an idea," April said, watching Clint.

"I am," he said, "but we might also need some men from Parker Kline."

"How many men are you gonna need for this idea?" Molly asked.

"A lot," Clint said, "a whole lot. . . . "

THIRTY-EIGHT

Parker Kline agreed to see Clint right away, having him shown right into his office.

"What can I do for you, Mr. Adams?" he asked.

"I'd like to take you up on your offer of help, Mr. Kline."

"Certainly. What do you need?"

"Some men."

"How many?"

"About half a dozen would do it."

"I have three or four men who are decent hands with a gun—"

"I don't need gun hands," Clint said, "I just need bodies."

"What do you have in mind?"

Quickly Clint outlined his plan. Kline listened patiently, nodding his head.

"Do you think it will work?"

"I've seen Dorsett in action," Clint said. "He

usually handles things himself."

"He has his own men, you know," Kline said. "You'll have to take Pullman out of the action."

"I've thought of that."

"When do you want to do this?"

"I'd like to do it tonight, but I don't think I can get it set up that quickly. We'll do it tomorrow."

"Are you going to let the sheriff in on this?"

Clint hesitated, then said, "I don't think so. I think I'll keep the sheriff in the dark."

"Why is that?"

Clint hesitated, wondering if he should say what he was thinking, then decided to go ahead.

"I think the sheriff is collecting his pay from too many different places."

Kline studied Clint for a few moments then smiled and shook his head.

"Don't be too hard on the sheriff, Mr. Adams. It's a thankless job."

"Maybe so," Clint said. "Still I don't think it would be wise to let him in on what we're going to do."

"You think he'd tell Dorsett?"

"I don't want to put temptation in his path," Clint said.

"Well, I can't say that I blame you."

"So how about it?" Clint asked. "Do I get those men?"

"When and where do you want them?"

THIRTY-NINE

Molly had offered Clint and April one room before he left, but Clint asked for two. That drew him a look from April, but she didn't say anything until later.

"Did Kline agree?" Molly asked when Clint returned.

"Yes. He'll give us six men."

"And I can give you four."

"That makes ten," Clint said.

"Eleven."

He turned and looked at April.

"Ten," he said. "You're not in on this."

"Like hell I'm not."

"Molly, could you excuse us?" Clint asked.

"Sure," she said. "Time for me to put in an appearance downstairs anyway."

Molly left her office and Clint turned and looked at April.

"Don't even try to talk me out of it," April said warningly.

"I don't have to try to talk you out of it," Clint said, "because you were never in it."

"If you think—"

"How can this plan possibly work if you're in The Dream Palace?"

"What better diversion could there be than me?" she asked.

"April, I have the diversion all planned," Clint said. "All you would be is a distraction *to* the diversion."

"That's not fair—"

"You're going to stay here with Molly," Clint said. "When I get Gladys out of The Dream Palace I'm going to bring her here, and I want her to see you."

"Clint—"

"What good would it do for me to get her out if Dorsett gets you back?"

She opened her mouth to argue, then closed it and thought a moment.

"You realize I'm right, don't you?"

She nodded.

"And you hate it."

She nodded again.

"But you'll stay here?"

"Yes, yes, I'll stay here."

"Good."

Clint kissed her on the forehead. April grabbed him around the neck and pulled his face down so she could kiss him.

"Why did you tell Molly to give us separate

rooms?'' she asked. ''Are you trying to save my reputation?''

''No.''

''Then what?''

''April, sit down.''

They sat together on the sofa and he took her hands.

''Wait,'' she said.

''For what?''

''I know what you're gonna tell me.''

''You do?''

''You don't want me to fall in love with you.''

''Well,'' he said, ''it would make things easier.''

''Clint, I know you've been with a lot of women.''

''April—''

''I can tell, you know? I've been with my share of men. You know that.''

''April—''

''Let me finish,'' she said. ''You're right, we should sleep in separate rooms. You're going to help me get away from Leo, and then you're going to be on your way. It's okay. I accept that.''

He stared at her for a moment and then said, ''Uh, okay.''

''Is that what you wanted to tell me?''

''I just, uh, yeah, that's what I wanted you to understand.''

''Okay,'' April said, standing up. ''I understand. Besides . . .''

''What?''

''I see the way you and Molly look at each other.''

''What?''

"It's okay," she said. "Molly's my friend, and so are you. It's okay."

Clint stared at April in disbelief. She reached down and cupped his chin in her hand.

"Did you expect me to get upset? Clint, you're a wonderful man and you're putting yourself in danger for me. All I feel is gratitude."

"That's it?"

She smiled at him.

"Do you expect every woman to fall in love with you?" she asked.

"No," Clint said, "not every woman."

"Good." She walked to the door. "I'm going to go to my room."

"Okay."

"I'm not going to come to your room, Clint. If you want me, you come to mine."

"Okay."

"If not . . . then good night."

He watched her leave, shaking his head. She was an amazing woman.

FORTY

Clint was still sitting in Molly's office when she came back up.

"Where's April?" she asked.

"She went to her room."

Molly sat behind her desk.

"Do you think your plan is going to work?" she asked.

"I think so."

Suddenly Molly started to laugh.

"What's so funny?"

"I was just thinking you could end up burning Leo's place down tomorrow."

"That wouldn't be so bad, would it?"

"It would put him out of business," Molly said. "Sounds good to me."

"Naw," Clint said. "Too many people could get hurt. I think we'll stick to the original plan."

"My men will be here in the morning," Molly

said. "You can go over the plan then."

"Good, good," Clint said. "I told Kline to have his men here early, too."

"Good," Molly said.

They sat there for a few awkward moments, staring at each other. He studied her face and found that he enjoyed looking at her. Although she wasn't as pretty as April, her face had more character. There were lines around her eyes but they looked good on her. In fact, Clint had a feeling this woman would look good for years to come, one of those women who would become even better looking as she got older.

"Can I ask you a question?" Molly asked then.

"Sure."

"Why are you doing this?"

"You mean trying to help April?"

"Yes. Are you in love with her?"

"No, I'm not in love with her, Molly."

"But you have had sex with her."

"Yes."

Molly smirked and said, "You've been with a lot of women, haven't you?"

"This week, you mean?"

She laughed.

"You know what I mean."

"I like women."

"Oh, and I'm sure they like you, too."

He didn't answer.

"A lot."

He still didn't answer.

"So," she said.

"What?"

"April's gone to bed?"

"I guess."

"What are you going to do?"

He shrugged.

"What would you normally be doing?" she asked him.

"Having a drink, playing some poker . . ."

"Picking out a woman?"

"Maybe."

"But you don't have to pick tonight, do you?"

"What do you mean?"

"April is probably waiting for you."

"April and I have come to an understanding."

"Which is?"

"I've agreed to help her because we've become friends," Clint said. "Our relationship is nothing more serious than that."

"So," Molly said, "if we wanted to have sex on top of my desk she wouldn't care?"

"That's right," Clint said. "She said that I'm her friend and you're her friend."

Molly looked surprised.

"You talked about this?"

"Well . . ."

"What did she say?"

"She said she saw the looks we've been giving each other."

Molly's eyebrows went up.

"Have you been giving me looks?"

"I didn't think so."

"Have I been giving you looks?"

Clint hesitated, then said, "I thought so."

Molly smiled.

"I was . . . and so were you."

"I was, huh?"

"Uh-huh, and you're doing it again."

"Am I?"

"Yes. Why don't you come over here?"

Clint stood up, wondering if she was teasing, or bluffing, determined to call her bluff.

He walked around her desk, took her by the shoulders, lifted her to her feet, and kissed her. The kiss went on for a long time and they were both breathless when it ended.

"You thought I was bluffing, didn't you?" she asked.

"Yes."

She smiled and swept the top of her desk clean with a sweep of her arm. She sat on the desk and lifted her skirts. He saw that she wasn't wearing any underwear.

"You planned this, didn't you?" he asked.

She grinned with great satisfaction and said, "Let's just say I was hopeful."

FORTY-ONE

Clint couldn't recall having seen anything as sexually arousing as Molly Haywood sitting on her desk with her dress pulled up around her hips. Her thighs were smooth and firm, and the patch of pubic hair between her legs was bushy and darker than the hair on her head. He could feel himself swelling and knew she was as excited as he was. He could smell her arousal.

"Call my bluff now," she said.

He put his hand on her right thigh and rubbed it with his palm. Her skin was smooth and he could feel the muscles beneath the skin. He moved his hand to her inner thigh and touched her pubic hair with his thumb. The entire time they were looking into each other's eyes, as if waiting for the other to call it off.

He pushed through the hair with his thumb and found her hot and moist. He ran the ball of his thumb along her vagina until he touched her clit. She caught her breath and closed her eyes, biting her lip as he ran his thumb around and around, rolling her, encircling her.

"Jesus," she said, lifting her butt off the desk, "God, that feels good . . ."

He continued to touch her until suddenly she reached out and undid his gun belt. She set it aside on the desk, then undid his pants. She pulled his trousers and underwear down until his penis, erect and pulsing, jutted free, and then she grabbed his waist and pulled him to her.

He reached around behind her, cupped her naked buttocks in his hands, and lifted her. Thrusting his hips forward, he entered her, and she gasped and held him tightly. As he felt her heat engulf him, he groaned and then began moving his hips back and forth, pulling her to him as he did so.

She leaned back, resting her weight on her hands and arms, and began moving with him, arching her back. She kept her eyes closed, gasping as he went deeper and deeper.

They continued on like that for some time, sweat beginning to cover both of them. At one point Molly undid the bodice of her dress, allowing her breasts to bob free. They were full and firm, with heavy undersides and wide, brown aureola. Clint leaned forward to kiss them and lick them in turn, causing her to gasp even louder. He wondered at that point about the unlocked door, and whether or not someone would walk in on them.

At another point he unbuttoned his shirt and removed it. Using his legs and feet he managed to totally remove his pants and underwear and kick them away. That left him naked but for his boots, which he couldn't do anything about at the moment.

"Wait, wait . . ." she said then.

"What . . . ?"

"I want to switch," she said. "Change position."

"Why?" he asked.

She laughed and said, "My butt is starting to kill me!"

He withdrew from her, and she got to her feet, hurriedly discarded her dress, and then leaned over the desk, presenting him with her sore butt.

"This way," she said, "hurry . . ."

She spread her legs for him. He stepped up, gripped her hips, slid his penis between her thighs and entered her from behind.

"Oooh, God, yes . . ." she moaned aloud.

She was leaning on her desk the long way, so she was able to reach out with her hands and grip the desk on either side as Clint drove into her from behind.

"Yes, yes . . ." she said, and repeated it with every thrust of his hips.

They were both covered with sweat and the room was filled with a mixture of scents—perspiration, heat, the smell of her arousal, the scent of his. . . .

Time stood still, or passed incredibly quickly, Clint wasn't quite sure which. He had no idea how long they were going at it, but she couldn't seem to get enough of him, and he felt the same way. The intensity of their excitement seemed to increase rather than decrease. She shuddered and cried out many times, and he was able to maintain his erection and keep from ejaculating until finally he could wait no more. With a cry that was more a roar than a loud groan, he gave in and exploded inside of her. As he did so, she cried out as another wave of pleasure coursed through her. There was a screech as the desk moved, scraping the floor. It was as if the desk cried out with them. . . .

"God," Molly said.

She was lying on her back on her desk, still naked. Clint was sitting across the room on the sofa, also naked, staring at her with great pleasure.

"That desk never looked so good," he said, "but it's a little crooked."

"We'll fix it later," Molly said, "when we're finished."

"Oh?" Clint said. "We're not finished?"

"Are you?"

Actually, he was not done. Looking at her lying naked on her desk was giving "rise" to renewed vigor. His penis was rising again.

She turned her head, looked at him and smiled.

"Ah, I see you're not," she said. "Good, because neither am I."

He stood up and walked to the door.

"Where do you think you're going?" she demanded.

He stopped at the door and turned the lock, then turned and walked back to the desk.

"The first time we were lucky," he said, approaching her. "This time I don't want to take any chances."

FORTY-TWO

Clint spent the night in Molly's room as they tried their best to exhaust each other. They finally succeeded and both of them fell asleep. Somehow they managed to wake up and get downstairs in time to have breakfast before all the men arrived.

While they were having breakfast, April Donovan came down to join them. She took one look at them and knew what they'd been doing all night.

"Well," she said, smiling at them, "at least one of us got a good night's sleep."

Clint thought again what an amazing woman she was.

She sat down to have breakfast with them, eggs and bacon and potatoes and biscuits, and lots of coffee. They were finishing up when the men started to arrive.

"Sam," Molly told her cook, "make lots more coffee for the men."

As the men arrived they were each given a cup of coffee and told to sit down. As they did so they started to talk among themselves.

"Who are your best two men?" Clint asked Molly.

"That'd be O. J. McCall and Deke Bates."

"Get them over here."

Clint explained to McCall and Bates that there was a man in a doorway across the street watching the place.

"I don't want him hurt or killed," he explained, "but we can't let him go back to Pullman or Dorsett and tell them about this meeting."

"How long do you need him out of action for?" McCall asked.

"Until this time tomorrow would do nicely," Clint said.

"You got it," Bates said.

"And then get back here."

"Right."

They left, and by the time the last of the men arrived they were back, reporting that the job was done.

"Where is he?" Clint asked.

"There's a root cellar under this place," Bates explained. "He's tied up in there."

"Okay," Clint said. "Good job. Take a seat."

Clint went to Molly and told her about the man in her cellar.

"Make sure someone checks on him every few hours," he said. "I don't want him dying down there."

"I'll take care of it."

"Good."

"Aren't Pullman and Leo going to wonder what happened to him?"

"Let them wonder," Clint said. "It'll keep their minds busy."

"All the men are here, Clint," Molly said.

"Good. I'll go over the plan with them. This could take some time so you better get even more coffee ready," he told her. "We're going to have to work carefully on the timing."

Molly instructed her cook to make more coffee. Clint stood up in front of the men, introduced himself, explained the situation to them, and then began to meticulously outline his plan for getting Gladys away from Leo Dorsett.

FORTY-THREE

"What is it?" Dorsett asked Pullman, as the man entered his office.

"It's Connelly, the man I had watching the Gold River."

"What about him?"

"He's gone," Pullman said.

"What do you mean, gone?"

"Just what I said. He's disappeared."

"You think Adams had something to do with it?"

"I do."

Dorsett sat back and made a disgusted sound.

"It wouldn't have happened if you'd gotten rid of Adams yesterday, would it?"

"He never came out of the Gold River," Pullman said, "and I wasn't about to go in there after him."

"Well, he's got to come out some time. Send

two men to watch the place this time, so they can watch each other's backs."

"I've already done that."

"Then get out! I have some thinking to do."

Pullman stared hard at Dorsett until the saloon owner began to fidget. Dorsett wondered if he could get the gun out of the desk in time, should Pullman decide to do something rash.

Pullman, for his part, made his final decision right there and then. This was the last job he'd do for Leo Dorsett.

Without a word to Dorsett, he turned and left the office.

Dorsett sat back in his chair and covered his face with his hands. He was worried about Gladys. The girl had not spoken to him all day yesterday; she had avoided him like the plague. If she talked . . .

Dorsett had undergone highs and lows this week. The high was having both Elsa and Gladys naked in his bed. He had fucked Elsa, making the girl cry out again and again, and then he'd had Gladys as well. It was afterward that he told Gladys to show Elsa how to please a man with her mouth. The black girl, who had cried after sex, had resisted, but a couple of slaps to the face had made her cooperative. She'd made him angry, though, and that was when he punched her. She was a little thing, with a thin neck, and it had snapped the second time he hit her with a closed fist. Then he'd had to hit Gladys to keep her from screaming.

Gladys was afraid of him, because she had seen him kill Elsa—but Dorsett was worried about her for that very same reason. What would happen if she decided to talk? Even after Pullman did away with Adams, Gladys could go to the sheriff. Osborne was on his payroll, but that didn't mean that he'd go along with murder.

Dorsett came to the decision that after Pullman took care of Adams, he was going to have to do something about Gladys. Pullman seemed dead set against violence when it came to women, but Dorsett thought that he could offer the man enough money to make it hard for him to resist.

Once Adams and Gladys were gone, Dorsett could bring April back into the fold, and everything would be as it was before.

Gladys—whose last name was Kane, although Leo Dorsett had never asked her that—sat in her room, naked on the bed, her knees drawn up to her chest, her arms wrapped around her knees. She sat that way for a long time. She hadn't slept well the last two nights. Every time she closed her eyes she saw Leo Dorsett beating that poor black girl to death. She was afraid that Dorsett would eventually do the same thing to her. After all, she had seen him commit murder. How long would it take him to decide to kill her, just to be safe?

How could she get out of this? If only she had spoken to April and Clint Adams when they came to see her, but she was too frightened then to speak.

Now she was too frightened not to, if only someone would ask her!

FORTY-FOUR

It took most of the day but Clint thought they finally had the timing down correctly.

Before they even worked on it, though, Clint had asked them all a question.

"How many of you are known on sight as working for your boss?"

None of them raised their hands immediately, and then a few men put them up tentatively. As it turned out, *some* of the men could be identified by *some* people. However, they all maintained that there was nothing unusual about any of them going to The Dream Palace. That established, they began to go over the plan, concentrating on the timing.

"All right," Clint said, looking the men over. "We've been at this all day. Get something to eat and be back here by six. I want to put this thing into play at seven."

The men stood up and started to file out. Molly had kept her place closed for the day, and a lot of customers had been turned away.

"Can I open now?" Molly asked.

"Sure," Clint said, "I don't want to put you out of business. When the men return, have them go around the back. I'll meet them there."

Molly nodded and went to tell her bartender, Dugan, to open. April came over, an apprehensive look on her face.

"Is this going to work, Clint?"

"Of course it's going to work, April," Clint said. "Look at all the preparation we've put into it."

She looked around at the men who were leaving the saloon.

"And this is all for me?" She seemed confused, as if she wondered why all these men would be gathering just to help her.

"For you," Clint said, "and for Elsa, April. Don't forget her."

"How can I?" she asked. "I see her every time I close my eyes."

"Just relax and wait for me to get back here later with Gladys. If we can get her to talk, all our problems will be solved."

"My problems, you mean," she said.

"We're friends," he said, giving her a hug, "and I've made your problems my problems."

"Yeah," she said, "but if anything goes wrong you're the one who's going to get hurt."

FORTY-FIVE

The only possible chink in the plan was that Clint felt he had to be there. If Dorsett or Pullman spotted him, that might put the plan in jeopardy—depending on their reaction. He felt he had no choice, though. It was his idea, and it wouldn't do to send everyone else in while he stayed outside. Besides, he wanted to be the one to grab Gladys and pull her out of there.

Clint's plan was for all the men to enter Leo Dorsett's Dream Palace over the course of a few hours, so that by the time the entertainment started they'd all be in position. He would be the last to enter.

It probably wasn't necessary to have so many men involved, but he wanted to be on the safe side. He didn't know how many men Dorsett and Pullman would have available. Some of the men were instructed to do nothing unless it looked as if the others were outnumbered and in danger.

Clint sat at a table at the Gold River with April and Molly, waiting for everyone else to get into position.

"It's time," he said finally.

Both women looked at him, and he knew what they were thinking.

"I'll be back soon," he said, "with company."

As Clint left the Gold River he saw the two men standing in the doorway across the street. That was not a problem. There had been nothing for them to see. Now they could follow him to The Dream Palace if they wanted to, and he didn't care.

Everything was in place.

"Good crowd," Jake the bartender said to Leo Dorsett as he set a beer in front of his boss.

"Yeah."

"Pullman's here."

"So?"

Jake looked down at Dorsett and asked, "Is there something I should know?"

"Just tend bar, Jake. That's your job."

Jake wanted to say he knew his job, but Dorsett didn't look like he was in the mood to be talked back to. He turned and went back to the bar. He knew something was going to happen tonight. As the bartender in one of the most popular saloons in town he knew almost everybody who lived here, and he knew that there were a lot of Parker Kline's men present, and a few of Molly Haywood's—and he doubted they were there for no reason.

It was when Clint Adams walked in, though,

that he really knew something was brewing—and he wanted no part of it. He was going to be ready to hit the floor at the first sign of trouble.

Clint entered The Dream Palace and walked to the bar.

"Hello, Jake."

"Mr. Adams."

Jake looked nervous, like he knew something was in the air. Clint hoped that no one else—least of all Pullman and Dorsett—were as observant.

"A beer, please."

"Comin' up."

Jake had just set the beer down when Pullman appeared at Clint's side.

"What are you doing here?" he asked.

"I came for the entertainment. Best in town, or hadn't you heard."

"I think you should come with me."

"I haven't finished my beer."

"Leave it."

Clint shook his head.

"Can't do it, Pullman. I already paid for it. I've got to drink it. Besides, the entertainment is about to start."

Pullman looked toward the stage where a woman—Clint recognized her as Alice—came out. The piano started up and she began to dance.

"After the girls," Pullman said, "you and me are taking a walk."

Clint smiled.

"I'll be right here," he lied.

Apparently, the customers were not letting April's absence affect their appreciation of a naked woman. They were clapping and stomping their feet. Some of the chief clappers and stompers were Kline and Haywood men. Clint hoped they wouldn't get so involved that they'd forget their jobs.

Clint looked around for Molly's man, O. J. McCall. He had a key role in what was about to happen. Clint noticed him standing near the piano, an unlit cigarette in his mouth. McCall caught Clint's eye but did not nod. That was good enough for Clint.

A succession of girls came out, dancing and removing their clothes, and Clint soon began to worry that maybe Gladys wasn't going to dance tonight. Her appearance onstage was supposed to set the whole plan in motion. Finally, though, just when he thought the last girl had danced, the blonde appeared onstage and everyone cheered enthusiastically. Apparently, she had already become a crowd favorite.

Clint straightened up and looked over to where Leo Dorsett was sitting at his table. The man was alone, and he was watching Gladys intently. He looked around further and located Pullman, who was watching Clint intently. He had no idea how many men Pullman had in the saloon, but he knew he needed to get the man's eyes off him when the action started.

Clint looked around for Deke Bates and found him. Bates was the other man with a key role, and that was to get Pullman's attention.

If everything went smoothly, Clint would be out of there with Gladys in a matter of minutes.

FORTY-SIX

As Gladys took her first step, things began to happen.

O. J. McCall struck a match, lit his cigarette, and then let the flame touch the edge of a piece of sheet music. The piano player was so intent on playing that he didn't notice until it was too late. The sheet music flared, and suddenly the wood of the piano caught.

That he noticed.

"Hey!" he shouted and stopped playing to try to extinguish the flames.

At the same time Deke Bates and one of Parker Kline's men started a fight. Deke hit the other man, who went stumbling back right into Pullman.

In another part of the saloon another fight started between a Haywood man and a Kline man.

Clint thought this would look less suspicious if and when someone tried to reconstruct the events.

The rest of Kline and Molly Haywood's men stood ready, in case they were needed.

Clint was already on the move toward the stage.

"You did that on purpose!" the piano player yelled at McCall.

"You're crazy!" McCall shouted.

Dorsett heard what was going on and saw the flames leaping from the piano.

"Jesus!" he shouted. He stood up and yelled, "Put that fire out before the whole place goes up!"

He looked around for Pullman and saw the man tangled up in a fight between two other men. He then became aware of several other fights in the room as some customers took the opportunity to join in the festivities.

Clint rushed the stage and looked up at Gladys. She stared down at him with frightened eyes.

"Gladys, do you want to get out?"

She hesitated, then nodded.

"Come with me, then."

He grabbed her hand and helped her down from the stage.

"Hey!" a man shouted. "Where you takin' her?"

Clint turned and as the man came at him he hit him in the jaw. More fights were breaking out, and the piano was ablaze now.

"We need a back way out," he said to Gladys.

"This way." She gripped his hand and took the lead, taking him to the door that led backstage.

• • •

A man burst into the sheriff's office and yelled, "Sheriff, they're burnin' down The Dream Palace!"

"What?"

Osborne jumped to his feet and followed the man outside. The man worked for Molly Haywood.

At the last minute Dorsett saw Clint Adams and Gladys go through the stage door and figured out what was going on. Ignoring the fire, he rushed over to Pullman and got him away from the fighting men.

"Adams is going out the back with Gladys. Stop him!"

Pullman looked around and saw that his men were engaged in fights. He grabbed the front of Dorsett's shirt.

"You're coming with me. We'll stop him together."

Dorsett didn't argue. He couldn't let Adams get away with Gladys.

"Let's go."

As Pullman and Dorsett came running out the front door of The Dream Palace, Sheriff Osborne saw them and knew something was happening.

"Sound a fire alarm," he called to Molly's man. Then he went to follow Pullman and Dorsett.

Gladys guided Clint to a back door that led to an alley behind the building. Because of a full moon there was enough light to see that to the right was nothing but a dead end. They turned left and as they did two men came into view.

Pullman and Dorsett.

Both had guns out.

"Hold it, Adams!" Pullman shouted.

"Where do you think you're going with that girl?" Dorsett demanded.

"I'm taking her to the sheriff, Leo."

"The sheriff?" Pullman asked, frowning. "What for?"

"Aren't you curious, Pullman, about why Leo is more concerned with losing this girl than his saloon, which is on fire?"

Clint couldn't see Pullman's eyes, but from the tilt of the man's head he could see that he was interested.

"It's because of the black girl, Elsa."

"Kill him," Dorsett said.

"What about the girl?" Pullman asked.

"You don't strike me as the kind of man who approves of beating women, Pullman," Clint said, "let alone killing them."

"What the hell are you talking about?" Pullman demanded.

"Kill them!" Dorsett shouted. "Kill them both!"

"Tell him, Gladys."

Gladys looked at Clint nervously, and he nodded.

"Mr. Dorsett killed that girl," she said finally. "He killed Elsa. He beat her to death with his fists."

Now Clint saw Pullman's body turn toward Dorsett.

"You sick son of a bitch!"

"Oh, come on, Pullman," Dorsett said. "You kill people."

"I don't kill women, Dorsett," Pullman said, holstering his gun. "If you want these two killed, do it yourself."

With that Pullman turned and started to walk away.

Dorsett's temper flared, as it had the other night with Elsa. He had the gun in his hand and he could have fired at Clint or Gladys, but Pullman was walking away from him, ignoring him, and he hated that.

As Dorsett turned, Clint knew he was going to shoot Pullman in the back. He couldn't allow that. He drew and fired in one swift motion and did to Dorsett what he had, for years, feared someone would do to him.

He shot *him* in the back.

Pullman whirled around at the sound of the shot, drawing his gun, but stopped when he saw Dorsett slump to the ground.

Clint left Gladys and walked to the fallen Dorsett.

"Much obliged," Pullman said to Clint.

"If any man deserved to be shot in the back," Clint said, as if justifying it to himself, "he did."

Pullman holstered his gun.

"I agree."

Suddenly, Sheriff Osborne walked in on the scene.

"Are we gonna have trouble, Sheriff?" Pullman asked.

"I heard everything," Osborne said, looking down at Dorsett.

"I'm leaving town, Sheriff," Pullman said. "Any objection?"

"None."

Without another word Pullman walked away.

The back door of the saloon opened and O. J. McCall came running out. He stopped short when he saw Dorsett on the ground with Clint and Osborne standing over him.

"The fire's out," he said to Clint.

"Good." Clint was glad. Burning down The Dream Palace was not his goal, and now April would be able to continue running it. She wouldn't have to work for anyone else.

"Gladys?"

The girl walked over to him.

"I think you'd better talk to the sheriff."

"A-all right."

"You're okay now," Clint said. He looked down at Leo Dorsett, the lowest form of man he'd ever run into. Not only had he beaten a defenseless woman to death with his bare hands, but he'd been about to shoot a man in the back. "It's all over now."

Watch for

THE OMAHA HEAT

164th novel in the exciting GUNSMITH
series from Jove

Coming in August!

If you enjoyed this book, subscribe now and get...

TWO FREE

A $7.00 VALUE—

If you would like to read more of the very best, most exciting, adventurous, action-packed Westerns being published today, you'll want to subscribe to True Value's Western Home Subscription Service.

Each month the editors of True Value will select the 6 very best Westerns from America's leading publishers for special readers like you. You'll be able to preview these new titles as soon as they are published, *FREE* for ten days with no obligation!

TWO FREE BOOKS

When you subscribe, we'll send you your first month's shipment of the newest and best 6 Westerns for you to preview. With your first shipment, two of these books will be yours as our introductory gift to you absolutely *FREE* (a $7.00 value), regardless of what you decide to do. If

you like them, as much as we think you will, keep all six books but pay for just 4 at the low subscriber rate of just $2.75 each. If you decide to return them, keep 2 of the titles as our gift. No obligation.

Special Subscriber Savings

When you become a True Value subscriber you'll save money several ways. First, all regular monthly selections will be billed at the low subscriber price of just $2.75 each. That's at least a savings of $4.50 each month below the publishers price. Second, there is never any shipping, handling or other hidden charges—*Free home delivery*. What's more there is no minimum number of books you must buy, you may return any selection for full credit and you can cancel your subscription at any time. A TRUE VALUE!